# DNA doesn't lie

Trudy M. Wassenaar

Cover illustration: Karoly Farkas, www.farkas.de

Other works by the author: 'An unusual job' (2014). www.booksbytrudy.com

ISBN 978-1-519-33996-6

# Acknowledgements

I thank my sister Annelieke for her encouragements and suggestions, and my editor Claudette Cruz for dotting the i's and crossing the t's. A special thank you to all those colleagues who have given me feedback that convinced me there is a niche for novels in which science plays an important role.

# DNA doesn't lie

# I

My winter depression was at a record low. When I was young I had never experienced this melancholy; every season had had its own attractions, and after the variable weather with storm, rain, fog and every possible type of precipitation that is typical for autumn, that lovely season with its spectacular colours and delicate, musky smells, the first winter weather had always given me a feeling of peace and compliance. I had loved the scenery of snowy fields and the nakedness of trees, as they stood black against a crisp blue sky, or the filigree artwork of hoarfrost after a cold night. Winter had been enjoyable, with its cosy long evenings, the season's holidays with lots of candles and sweets and guests attending copious dinners; with hot chocolate after long, cold walks and a satisfying drowsiness after skating and skiing excursions. I had loved the darkness of winter as much as I had loved the revitalizing power of spring, the heat of summer, and the beauty of autumn.

Not anymore. It seemed winter lasted longer with every year I grew older. Generally, in my perception time seemed to pass faster with increasing age. When I thought of the endless days of childhood, when a week lasted forever and a year took an eternity to pass… nowadays the months and years just flew by, and beyond the age of fifty, time seemed to hurry up with a devilish pleasure. (*Over fifty years old – more than half a century! Most likely I had fewer years ahead of me than I had lived! No, don't think about it, Sue, don't make it worse.*) This subjective quickening of time seemed to halt itself in winter, in particular in January, a month in which nothing happened and time stretched itself, as if to make up for the acceleration caused by age. By the time the last festive dinner remains had been thrown away and cleaning the living room no longer recovered needles that the Christmas tree had shed, a persistent emptiness and sadness settled in. Although by this time mid-winter had passed, one could still barely notice the days were getting longer. Every morning, dawn seemed to delay itself, and on cloudy days it didn't even get completely light. January sucked!

I told myself it could be worse. I was living in Germany, where our little village was located at nearly precisely 50 degrees latitude, which is a long way south of the Arctic Circle. People living further up north, in Scandinavia, say, or Canada or Siberia experienced far shorter days in winter, and might not see any daylight for weeks, so I told myself they had far more reason to feel miserable, and I shouldn't complain. It didn't help resolve my winter depression. My suffering wasn't less because other people suffered more – that was no consolation at all.

I told myself there was a plausible explanation for my depression, namely lack of bright light, especially in the morning. Waking up while it was still dark for weeks at a time put my biological clock out of phase with the hours of the day, which resulted in either a serotonin deficiency in the brain, or a melatonin deficiency (the experts couldn't agree on the actual physiological cause of winter depression), but, either way, as soon as the days would lengthen a bit more and I was exposed to longer stretches of sunlight, my spirits would rise. I knew this. But it was of little comfort and it certainly didn't make me feel any better.

My mood got even worse when I thought of work, or rather, the lack of it. I am a self-employed scientist, and try to make a living as a research consultant. This winter there had been a severe dip in my assignments, which combined an empty calendar with short days and miserable, wet weather (if only it would freeze, with clear skies so that the sun would be out, I wouldn't mind the cold so much!), into a sickening cocktail that made me extremely miserable.

It wasn't the first time I had run out of jobs for a while. When this happened in other times of the year, I had used the opportunity to work in the garden, or go on long biking tours. Those weeks of occupational inactivity had offered a welcomed window to recharge the batteries, enabling a start with double energy on the next job that offered itself. But what to do in winter? Even my regular visits to the gym had suddenly halted as the building was closed because of a defect with their heating system. Lack of physical activity made my depression worse. I wished I could hibernate, curl up under a blanket and sleep till winter was over.

It was in this terrible state of mind that I received an unexpected email that changed everything.

***

Checking my email had been a torment these past few weeks, wading through loads of spam messages that had slipped through my spam filter, notices of expensive scientific meetings I didn't want to or couldn't afford to attend (if such invitations weren't a scam; one couldn't be certain these days), and invitations to send a manuscript to journals I had never heard of. I was longing for news from my regular clients, a new assignment, a novel challenge, whatever job to do. Late afternoon of this mid-January Thursday, when I opened my email inbox with twenty-three new messages, expecting all of them to be equally boring, I discovered a real message amongst them, and it turned out to be a jewel. The mail that raised my spirits by several magnitudes was an invitation from a respected publisher of scientific journals and books. They asked me if I was willing to write a book; they had identified me as a potential author based on my publication record, which I was sure they had checked on the Internet. The subject of the book they envisaged was the use of DNA techniques in forensic investigations. The provisional title they proposed was 'Advantages of Molecular Techniques in Forensics', a sufficiently vague and generic title to propose to an author, who could interpret it this way or that to fit his or her expertise.

I was realistic enough to know that I was probably not the first and only scientist they had contacted. More likely, they had already gone through a list of candidate writers (though I hoped I was not too far down their list...), asking one at a time, expecting a negative answer until one would take the bait. Publishers know that scientists are busy, and writing a scientific book consumes an awful lot of time. Only few individuals are prepared to take up such a huge task. He or she has to be an expert on the requested subject, and be willing to spend many hours reading through scientific literature, in order to fill in any remaining knowledge gaps, and to ensure inclusion of the latest advances in the field. One should be efficient and inclined to work long hours in order to combine all this work with ongoing tasks, and a certain degree of narcissism would probably also be needed to say yes to an invitation like this. Why else would one commit oneself to such a task? Fair enough, to be an author of a scientific book looks good on your CV (in case you're thinking of changing jobs), and can open future professional opportunities. But most of all, one has to enjoy writing. My guess was that most authors liked to write about their work.

I considered my options. I was an expert in this field, and was relatively well informed on the latest scientific progress in forensic DNA investigations. I was willing to deepen my knowledge by reading through the subjects I was not completely up-to-date with, which would not only produce a better book, but would also be a personal advantage for future commitments. Moreover, I had the time; right now I had lots of time. And, finally, they would pay a reasonable fee. It wouldn't pay well if you summated all the hours I would have to invest, but it meant I wouldn't be without an income for the next couple of months. On the negative side… actually, I couldn't think of any negative consequences. The worst that could happen would be that once I had agreed on the task, a number of other assignments might offer themselves so that I would become swamped with work. That wouldn't necessarily be bad. I always felt at my best if I had a lot on my plate. And from experience I knew (this wasn't the first book I would write) that a publisher could be put on hold: their deadlines were flexible, if needed.

With raised spirits I started writing a response to the invitation email, which took me more than an hour, while I brainstormed about the kind of book I would like to write. The publisher had not explicitly stated what target readers they had in mind, leaving me free to consider the options. I didn't want to produce a methodology book, in which would be 'presented and reviewed' the types of methods currently in use in forensic laboratories. Such an approach would result in what I disrespectfully regarded as a cookbook with recipes how particular experiments should be performed. There were a number of such books on the market already; and although a novel methodology book would sell for a couple of years, as methods change over time and the latest book available is usually the one that sells best, eventually a newer book would inevitably be released to replace all existing ones, including mine. My main objection against a methodology book was, however, that scientists working in forensics were usually stubborn, and would prefer their own optimized, qualified, standardized and accepted methods. I didn't want to preach changes that were hardly going to be implemented.

Instead, I envisioned a book explaining the pros and cons of DNA techniques and their applications to people who would have to work with the results of such investigations, not performing them with their own hands in a lab. I was thinking of the judges, lawyers, legal officers, police inspectors, and politicians who often did not have a degree in science, and had probably never seen the inside of a laboratory, but who had to deal with scientific evidence produced on a lab bench. They should be sufficiently informed about the advantages and disadvantages, the strengths and weaknesses, the hurdles and pitfalls that could be involved in DNA evidence. I considered them a more important reader audience than the scientists who actually performed the experiments, and I knew that lack of understanding of the science behind DNA evidence could easily result in misinterpretation, potentially resulting in miscarriage of justice. There had been some hilarious cases of that in the past that could serve as excellent examples in the book I envisaged.

It would be a challenge: explaining such complex material to readers without much background in biology, genetics or biochemistry, not to forget the difficult statistical aspects that were so important in this field. The newspapers often wrote about 'evidence with a certainty of one in a million' as if that meant those were the odds that the culprit was guilty. Lack of understanding of the statistical value behind a match in a DNA comparison had frequently resulted in wrong judgements. Come to think of it, journalists could also benefit from the book whose contents were taking shape while I reflected on my response letter.

A recent case of homicide in our local town came to my mind. A young woman had been found strangled in her bed. The fact that she had been found naked, that she had lived in an expensive apartment in one of the better quarters of the city, and that she had been an astonishing beauty added to the popularity of the story. The press was full of the murder, sympathizing with the victim (photographs of her pretty face in better days were all over the papers) and condemning the person who had killed her, speculating on various scenarios, amongst which a *crime passionnel* was the most popular. The story took a different turn when a journalist revealed that she had worked as a prostitute. The press sneered that it would be hard to identify the murderer based on DNA evidence, since she would likely have had a number of customers before the one who had finished her. The ignorance! Few prostitutes worked without a rubber these days, and a woman living in such a posh place would be active in the upper section of her profession, where it was even less likely to do it without a condom. Besides, sperm was not the only source for a DNA trail, while a proper investigation could ensure that any samples collected at the crime scene were likely to be related to the murderer, and not to other visitors who had at some time visited her place. Since the revelation of her profession, the story had no longer hit the headlines. I pondered on how the press would have handled the story in case the woman had been less attractive, had lived in a cheaper place, or had had a different means to earn an income. Did any of that matter, I wondered, did one or the other circumstance make the murder worse, or less cruel? Not in my opinion: whoever had killed her should be caught and put behind bars when sane, or in a closed institution when not, if only to prevent him (it was unlikely her killer had been a she) from killing other women, prostitutes or not. Journalists should report such cases with a bit more professionalism, and a basic knowledge of forensic investigations could help them with that.

I phrased my thoughts in the email response to the publisher, then pressed 'save' instead of 'send'. I was going to sleep over this, and would look at it again tomorrow, and probably revise my answer over the next few days, until I was satisfied with my proposal. There was no need to respond in a hurry. The next one on the publisher's list of potential authors would not be contacted in at least another month's time. I was going to send my positive response in a few days, and then we would negotiate over the contract, while I could draft an outline and a table of contents, and start browsing through some literature just for a start… My natural enthusiasm returned with every hour I thought about this, and quickly replaced the clouds of depressive fog.

It felt good to be alive.

Satisfied, I poured myself a glass of wine, anticipating the pleasure of telling my husband this news-of-the-day. I knew he would be happy for me. Because of his demanding job as a professor in Physics, Robert's typical complaints concerned the opposite, as he was frequently too busy to enjoy life, instead of having too little to do. But he recognized my frustration, as he would also be unable to cope with being under-challenged. He had authored a number of physics books (which actually sold better than any of mine…) so he knew what would be involved in my new commitment. His professorship at the university had been the reason why we had left our beloved England to go live in Germany. Our two boys were born here, and, unlike their parents, spoke German without an accent, though at home the family conversed in English. They were both studying now and no longer lived with us. My husband worked long hours and travelled a lot, and as a consequence I spent most of my time alone at home. Now I was looking forward to enjoying those long hours at my computer again, instead of hanging on the couch in low spirits.

The buzz of my smartphone startled me. My husband informed me, by means of a text message, that he would stay in town for dinner and expected to be in late.

Instead of a meal for two I only had to cater for myself, then. Heating up a few leftovers from the fridge would do. Celebrating the end of my winter dip was no fun on my own, so after another glass of wine I decided to go to bed. Tomorrow I would make an early start, sorting out a few things that I had obstinately refused to do because of my bad mood these past weeks. I would make a clean sweep in order to spend all my energy on the book; I could hardly wait now before I would get started!

## II

The negotiations with the publisher had gone smoothly, and within a fortnight a contract was signed. I had spent many hours already behind my computer, browsing through the literature that was available from specialized online libraries. For my work I was extremely grateful for PubMed, the extensive online service provided by the US National Library of Medicine: a database containing the titles and often the abstracts of millions of scientific works; for many of these articles their full text was freely accessible. PubMed was my main source of information whenever I started a new project.

The more I read, the more I was convinced my book would be a valuable addition to existing literature. There seemed to be a gap between highly specialized, technical books that went into extreme detail at one end of the spectrum, and general educational books that only touched upon subjects at the other. I could imagine the difficulties professionals would encounter if they had to deal with DNA evidence in court without the necessary scientific background. They would be completely dependant on external experts, without a chance to evaluate their expert opinions. It was currently hard for them to obtain relevant, concise and unbiased information required to form their own opinion. It was my intention to fill in the gaps left by other authors. It further struck me that forensic techniques were mostly presented in a way as if problems and complications were hardly ever encountered, pretending that experiments never failed and every outcome was infallible. I knew from experience that this impression didn't represent real life. In a lab, things frequently go wrong, and Murphy's Law might well be the law most frequently cited unofficially in a scientific environment. Problem-solving is part of the profession; it composed a major part of the activities I did for a living. It would only be fair to describe the real difficulties encountered in a forensic laboratory, including the limitations and uncertainties of the evidence put to court.

I had started researching for my book and drafting outlines and concepts with such a frenzy that the outside world no longer existed. I hardly noticed it when the weather changed, and winter finally presented itself with its cold and impressive serenity. One morning, when I opened the front door to put the rubbish outside (noticing that the door had not been properly locked the evening before), it was a shock to see how much snow had fallen. A watery sun brightened up the world while I cleared the pavement in front of our house. Happily, I noticed I no longer depended on sunlight to feel good. A fire burned inside me that kindled my energy. An alarm clock was no longer needed to wake up early, and these days I had to force myself to break away from my desk and go to the gym (which fortunately had reopened) in order to get some exercise.

Eventually, I had emptied most of my freezer, as I had been too occupied to cook dinner. The fact that my husband had been away to attend an international meeting this past week had made it even easier to lose myself with work.

Now that Robert was back, and I had run out of supplies, it was time to take a break to stock up. I cleaned the snow off the car (not an easy task, as it had recrystallized during the cold nights and was now more like a frost-ice cover) and made a trip to the city. My car radio switched on automatically, broadcasting a discussion programme about local politics. The recent murder case of that prostitute, who was called Lena Lotus (I reckoned that was her professional pseudonym) was back as a news item, and it had opened Pandora's box. Journalistic research had revealed that at least one local politician had been amongst her clients. I wondered how the journalist had obtained that information; had a member of the investigation team leaked? On the radio a panel of 'experts' was now discussing whether a politician is still trustworthy if he uses such services. It didn't matter that the man was a bachelor, and that prostitution is legal in Germany (like everybody else, Lena would have had a health insurance and would have paid taxes over her income). The opposition had smelled blood, and they were going to sacrifice their victim! The discussion on the radio didn't make much progress during my twenty-minute drive into the city, and I wasn't sorry to switch it off when I had reached my destination.

Absentmindedly I pushed my trolley up the slightly sloping path of the supermarket, with every step crushing grit that had been strewn on the slippery snow to avoid accidents, when I nearly bumped into a young woman who was leaving the store. It turned out to be a former colleague of mine, Monica Malzberger. I had not seen her for a long time.

"Well, that's a surprise, Monica! *Wie geht's dir*? How nice to see you!" I exclaimed, halting abruptly to avoid a collision of our shopping trolleys.

"Dr. Swanson, a surprise indeed! How are you?" Her answer had been friendly enough, but her smile was forced and her eyes didn't smile with the lower part of her lovely face.

Monica had been a lab technician in the research group I had worked with a few years ago. She was in her mid-twenties, and I remembered her as one of the most talented members of our technical staff, bright and with that skill I can only describe as 'golden hands': every experiment she performed worked out perfectly. Her results were always spotless, precise and reproducible. Combined with her modesty she had been a joy to work with; I had managed to break through her shyness and we had really liked each other. Such a talented person was hard to keep, and indeed she had been offered an opportunity for promotion that she had not turned down. She had moved to the most prestigious laboratory in the city, which, by coincidence, happened to be a forensic lab. Since her farewell party two years ago, we had not seen each other.

"What brought you back in this part of town? How is life treating you? How's the job... no, wait, too many questions at once. Let me do my shopping quickly and then we'll go for a coffee, I hope you have time for that? You'll be my guest, of course!" I rattled away. Suddenly I realized I had not socialized for two weeks, and I craved a moment of leisure with a friend. I remembered how pleasant the coffee breaks had been I had spent with Monica together, and how much fun those odd late nights had been that we had spent in the lab, when experiments that couldn't be halted extended our working hours into the early morning... it would be nice to have a chat with her.

With a slight hesitation, which I couldn't help noticing, Monica agreed to meet in half an hour in the lunchroom down the street.

***

While I was stowing my groceries away in the back of my car I thought of Monica. She had joined the research group directly after she had finished her education, before I became a member of staff of that group. By the time I got on board she had already earned the reputation of the most reliable technician in the team. Despite her skills, she had remained a modest and pleasant little girl. She had not revealed much of her private life (in my experience most Germans keep their private life strictly separate from their occupational environment); all I knew was that her parents lived in this city, and that she had a boyfriend, at least she had been in a relationship at that time. She was a petite brunette with a soft voice; she was gentle, shy and sweet. Monica was not particularly pretty, but her eyes had a melancholic expression that some men would find very attractive. She had not changed much since I had last seen her, other than that the sadness in her eyes had magnified. I wondered if something tragic had happened in her life recently.

I took a seat in the *Wintergarten* of the lunchroom, a spacey glass-and-wood extension that was heated in winter. From here one had a nice view over the snow-covered fields, with the slowly spinning windmills performing their synchronic ballet at the hilltop beyond the valley. After a few minutes Monica joined me, taking off her coat while she took her seat. I was glad to see she was prepared to spend some time with me.

"It has been a long time since we last met. I think it was at your farewell party… I'm sorry I have not been in touch since," I apologized. I was notoriously negligent when friendships were concerned. I never seemed to find the time to call my friends, or pay them a visit, and when I did have the time (as I did, only a few weeks ago) I didn't fancy seeing anybody. I was a difficult person to stay friends with, and I was very aware of my flaw.

"Oh, don't worry, I'm sure you have been very busy," was her polite reply. She was trying to keep the conversation neutral. It had been too long since we had last talked; our ways had separated and we were no longer close.

The waitress came to take our order: coffee and cake for me, and green tea for my guest – she didn't want to have anything to eat.

"So what brought you back here?" I asked, to break the ice.

"I moved back in with my parents. They are both retired now, and travel a lot. They needed someone to look after the dog, tend the house and garden and keep an eye on things. So I decided to come back. It's OK, you know…" The last remark sounded somewhat like an apology, though I didn't quite understand what there was to apologize for. Maybe her relationship had broken up, and that had made her say it was OK. It was not my business to ask for details. We chatted some about the sudden change of the weather, and how every year the traffic had to adjust to winter conditions, as if most drivers had forgotten how to behave on snowy roads. A brief silence passed. Had I said something stupid? Had there been a traffic accident in her family, maybe? Since it was work that had connected us, I changed our conservation to what I considered was a safe subject.

"So tell me, how's life in forensics?"

Monica dropped her gaze and swallowed. *Wrong choice, Sue!* I thought. I should have tried a different subject.

"Actually, I am no longer working at the Forensic Institute." She responded with an effort to let it sound calm.

"Oh, I'm sorry, I didn't know. You know, I regained an interest in forensics recently, as it is the subject of a book I have just started with," I quickly needed to divert the awkward subject to safer grounds, "mind, it's not going to be a methodological collection. I'm preparing an aid for those who use the lab evidence in court, you know, judges and lawyers and the like. Some of them hardly know what they are talking about." Monica pulled her face into a grin to acknowledge she was aware of the ignorance of some of them. In her professional life she would not have had to deal with lawyers or judges, though. Once her experiments were finished, the results would be put into an examiner's report by her supervisor, who would present it in court if needed. That was not her task. But the lack of understanding of the readers of those reports had been a regular subject of the lab's coffee table's conversation.

We chatted a while about life in this neighbourhood. She had lived here as a child, she told me, moving to this city with her parents when she was five. She had studied at the local *Technische Hochschule*, a technical university where she had absolved her education as laboratory assistant.

As the conversation continued, the distance between us diminished, and we started to feel connected again. We gossiped about our former colleagues, discussed the latest plan for a motorway extension (which received a lot of protests from local citizens of the NIMBY kind), and eventually it was safe for me to ask what I had wanted to know the moment she had told me she had left the forensic lab:

"So where do you work now, if I may ask?" Monica looked up to me, with those melancholic eyes, while she softly answered:

"I am still looking around. It isn't easy to find a job these days." I was really sorry for her. What a shame, what a waste of talent! I promised to let her know in case I heard of a vacancy somewhere.

"If you need a letter of reference, let me know. You know I have a high opinion of your skills," I reassured her.

"I'm not sure if I still deserve that," was her strange response. What was that supposed to mean?

"Monica, listen. I don't know what has happened in your past job, but I recognize professionalism when I see it. You have what I call golden hands, I know from experience you're very capable to work independently and reliably, your experiments were always perfectly planned and performed. You should be proud of your skills, and use the talents you have. You are born for lab work." I meant it.

She thanked me with a feeble smile. I would have loved to dig deeper, to find out what the reason was for her sudden insecurity, but that would have been inappropriate.

We chatted some more, and after about an hour we parted. I asked for her new telephone number, in case I heard of a job opportunity, and promised I would contact her soon. I realized with a pang that my promise was probably meaningless, and that she knew this. I was a lousy friend-keeper.

On my way home I digested our conversation. She had not said so, but I suspected that she had lost her job involuntarily. Either her temporary contract had not been renewed, or she had been forced to resign. I couldn't imagine how that could have happened. I promised myself to try and help Monica in whatever way I could; she was such a nice girl! There were a number of colleagues I could write, to ask if they happened to have a vacancy. It was the least I could do for her.

***

That afternoon my husband called me that he wouldn't be home for dinner. This had happened frequently lately. I didn't quite know what business he had in town that required such late nights so often. We didn't check each other's whereabouts. A little beginning of a worry settled somewhere in the back of my mind. I had noticed that he was frequently absent-minded, and he didn't seem to be himself lately. After a marriage of over twenty-five years, the passion that once was had faded, which I considered unavoidable. But right now we went through a phase in which there was very little warmth in our relationship and I didn't like the way this was going. I needed to talk to him about it someday, if a suitable occasion offered itself.

With a mood that could have been better I decided I had done enough for the day and made myself a salad. It was good to eat something fresh and green for a change. I would make myself a foam bath, read a book and make it an early night. Robert could stay away all night if he wished; I wasn't going to be bothered! My plan to have an early night didn't quite work out that way, as I tossed in bed for over two hours, but eventually I did fall asleep and didn't wake up when Robert came home.

# III

Next morning we had breakfast as if everything was all right. I didn't ask Robert how late he had come home, or where he had been, and he didn't provide an explanation voluntarily. I wondered if he noticed that I didn't ask. Probably not, men are not that sensitive, at least not the man I had married. The only words he spoke were that he had noticed the lock of our front door wasn't working properly, and could I please have someone look at that. I grunted a vague promise that I would take care of it. In lack of a conversation, I listened to the morning news on the radio. There had been another murder in our city this past weekend. The victim was called Laila (her surname was not released). The police wouldn't give any details yet, but from the snippets of information it seemed this was a case similar to that of the young woman Lena, who had been found dead eight weeks ago. The media were quick to point out resemblances between the two cases, and two hypotheses were being presented that I both considered unlikely. One journalist speculated that it was the work of a serial killer. Another hinted at links to politics, and speculated that the murder had been commissioned, to protect the reputation of certain influential persons. I was sceptical there would be a connection at all. The police would check extensively for similarities, but it was far more likely that these were unrelated incidents than that the two cases were connected. A thorough forensic investigation could shed light on this. I made a remark to the teacup in my hand that the police now had enough to do, and that I hoped they wouldn't make mistakes.

"I wish my book had been published already and they had read it, it could reduce the chance they screw up." Robert didn't look up from his Ipad on which he had been reading a British newspaper. His '*Hm*' could mean that he had heard me and acknowledged the value of my writings, or that he hadn't even registered what I was talking about. After a few seconds he added:

"You're making progress, then?" So he had noticed.

"It's a huge task, you know, but the introduction is coming along nicely," I replied.

I had written an extensive introduction for a non-specialist reader, starting with an explanation of what DNA is, what physical properties it has, how the DNA of people differs between individuals and how this can be determined experimentally. There was still an enormous task ahead of me, but at least I had a beginning.

***

One of the colleagues I had contacted as a result of my meeting with Monica responded a few days later that he had a temporary position available for a lab assistant because a member of his team would soon go on maternity leave. In Germany, many young mothers opt for *Erziehungsurlaub*, a period of up to three years in which they can stay home to look after their kids, while their job is secured. The employer can fill the post temporarily with a replacement, until the young mother returns to work. It wasn't a permanent job that I could mention to Monica, and the payment would be less than the job she had just left, but it was better than unemployment. I dug up the piece of paper she had scribbled her telephone number on and rang her up while I was enjoying a cup of coffee.

"Good morning, Monica, I have good news for you: I may have found you a temporary job. *Schwangerschaftsvertretung*, would you be interested? It is at the local University, in Hanzl's group, you know, the Genetics Department, so you wouldn't have to move. If you want to I can write you a letter of recommendation."

Her response was not as welcoming as I had expected.

"That's awfully kind of you, Dr. Swanson, but before you write that letter I believe we need to talk. *Wir müssen reden.* There is something you should know. When would you have time to meet me?"

I was taken aback. What was going on with that girl?

"I'm planning to visit the gym tomorrow, if you want I could combine that with a trip into town. What if we meet at 5 p.m., same place as last time?" She had made me curious now. I couldn't wait to learn what she wanted to tell me.

Monica accepted my suggestion and ended the call, leaving me standing in the kitchen frowning and slightly worried.

Not knowing what to think of this, I decided to put the subject aside for the moment and concentrated on my book. During the rest of the day I worked undisturbed, but for late that afternoon, when the telephone rang, by the sound of it, from the kitchen. I had forgotten to put it back on its charger on my desk, next to my computer. How stupid of me! The same had happened two days ago, when I had hurried to answer the call, only to hit my toe with a terrible force against the kitchen table. It had hurt badly; even now I felt it when I walked, and all that suffering for a call that had been a dialling mistake. This time I took more care where to put my feet while I hurried towards the phone. When I answered the call, there was silence on the other end of the line.

"*Hallo!* Sue Swanson!" I repeated clearly and in a demanding tone, but there was not a sound. I waited a few more moments and then hung up. Taking the phone back to my office to place it on its charger, I wondered how people could be so rude to remain silent after they misdialled. If that was what this call had been… The other day, when my toe met the table leg so unpleasantly, it had been a woman's voice apologizing that she had dialled the wrong number. Her number had not shown on the display, indicating that she was on an anonymous line not allowing a call-back service. This call now was again from an unknown number. Was it the same woman? Was the call maybe intended for Robert (whose surname was Callighan, while I had kept my maiden name, which is rather uncommon in Germany and was often the cause of confusion), and did the person not know he lived with a Sue Swanson? *Come on, Sue, you're imagining things.* The last call had been Monday, now it was Thursday. There was nothing in common here. Although both calls had occurred around seven. Last Monday… what about last Monday? Ah, yes, Robert hadn't come home for dinner. Well, that happened a lot these days. *No connection, Sue!* Nevertheless, I wasn't completely unprepared when, half an hour later, Robert indeed called to apologize that he had to stay in town and wouldn't come home for dinner. I wished I could convince myself that this was truly unrelated to the anonymous call.

***

When I met Monica the next day, she started her story with an apology.

"Dr. Swanson, I'm sorry I take up your valuable time. I know I shouldn't bother you with my problems, but it was your remark, the other day, that you are working on a book on forensics that got me thinking. The thing is, I lost my job at the Forensic Institute because of some unexplainable result that I had obtained, and my supervisor refused to accept it. I thought, maybe you can… I mean, with all your expertise, I don't know, maybe there is an explanation, after all."

She was clearly nervous. She was not used to admitting errors, to account for inaccuracies. She had always been in control of her doings. This was *terra incognita* for her, I could tell from her unfinished sentences.

"Why don't you start with explaining what kind of experiments you're referring to, and what results you got?" I calmly said.

"It was related to this woman who had been killed, you remember? I mean Lena, of course, not the woman from last week. We had received hair samples from the *Tatort*. As you know, we're not supposed to know the case to which our samples belong, but in this case it was obvious. We received three hair samples, for which I produced the fingerprints. Strangely, all three fingerprints were different. My negative controls were negative, so no contamination. I repeated the PCR, but I got the same result. I repeated it a third time to be absolutely certain, and then I reported that the three hairs belonged to different individuals. Really, there was no overlap beyond 30%, which you know is way below the threshold!"

I knew what she meant. Three hairs had been collected from the crime scene that could potentially belong to the murderer. They must have been found on, or close to the body. Monica would have received them in individual, sterile, DNA-free sample bags. She would have taken them out with clean pincers, to cut the root end of each hair into a tube with clean scissors. The DNA from the owner of those hairs could be extracted from that fragment with the use of organic solvents, but it would only recover a tiny amount of DNA, too little to work with. (Hair fragments that had been detached from the root were even harder to work with, as they contained even less DNA). So Monica had performed an experiment called PCR, short for Polymerase Chain Reaction. It is a way to produce many copies of a piece of DNA, by means of an enzyme called DNA polymerase. The technique had been invented by Kary B. Mullis, who had received the 1993 Nobel Prize in

Chemistry for his discovery. PCR can be used for many applications. The beauty of it is that it can produce thousands of copies of DNA strands from as little as one molecule to start with. However, this DNA production is so powerful that any DNA present as contamination would be copied as well. One has to take utmost care to avoid contamination of the sample, both during DNA extraction and during the PCR reaction.

In addition to the three hair samples that Monica had analysed in her PCR experiment, she would have added a tube in which all components of the reaction were present, but no hair DNA. The idea of this control is that if there is no DNA to start with, no copy DNA can be produced, so at the end of the experiment the tube remains negative. (In addition to this negative control Monica would also have added a positive control, in which a bit of known DNA is added to a tube, which is expected to produce a product, to make sure everything works as should be). A negative control should remain negative, in other words, no DNA copies should be found at the end of the experiment in that tube, but that isn't always the case. If any of the components of the reaction had been contaminated with foreign DNA, say from a skin cell (caused by an unintended touch of a pipette tip by a finger, for instance), the negative control would come up positive, and the results of the whole analysis would be discarded. But Monica trusted her results: *'My negative controls were negative'* were her words.

The DNA that she had copied from the three hairs had been analysed by electrophoresis to produce bands, and the combined banding pattern is called a 'DNA fingerprint' (it has nothing to do with fingers, but that's the term that has been coined for these banding patterns). Each individual will have his or her own DNA, and all cells from that individual will produce the same DNA fingerprint. Different individuals, on the other hand, produce different banding patterns. A few bands may, by coincidence, be of the same length, but the combination of seven, eight or more bands that are typically analysed in forensic applications are hardly ever the same between two individuals. The similarity between banding patterns is compared by computer analysis, and a threshold is chosen above which two patterns are said to be 'matching'. The three hair samples had produced three different banding patterns in Monica's experiment, and their degree of 'similarity' was reported as 'below 30%', which is the way the computer says the patterns were completely different.

"OK, so you produced three different patterns. No big deal, is it? The three hairs must have come from three individuals. Knowing the profession of the victim, it is not surprising that stains from different individuals were found in her apartment. What was the problem with that?"

Monica sighed.

"Nothing, in my opinion. But my supervisor, Dr. Kazinski, didn't accept my results. He said this was extremely unlikely, and he blamed me of sloppiness. He argued that all three hairs had probably been found on the body of the victim and there was no evidence for more than one *Täter*. So he took me off the case and ordered the PCR to be repeated by someone else. And when a colleague of mine repeated it, she got one pattern only. You got it?"

"Her positive and negative controls were OK, though?"

"Perfect. She had produced one and the same fingerprint from each of the three hairs, whereas I had produced three different patterns. Guess which result was considered correct?"

If I had been in charge, I would not have believed one or the other, but would have asked for more repetitions until I could explain the differences in the results. But her supervisor preferred to believe the better-fitting result that her colleague had produced and rejected Monica's work, without seeking an explanation for the discrepancy. I didn't know this Dr. Kazinski, other than his name. He was the current director of the Forensic Institute, but I had never had anything to do with him. I had worked with his predecessor until a couple of years back, when my contact with that lab ended. Right now I didn't understand Kazinski's motivation to reject the first experimental finding, and understood even less of his choice to believe the other. Had he been put under pressure by some Chief Inspector who was looking for one murderer, not three?

"Monica, how do you explain the different outcomes?" I asked. She shrugged.

"I thought about it for weeks, but there is no logical explanation. Gudrun got three tubes with the same fingerprint while I had produced that one only once, and she didn't get the two others that I got. It can't be, and yet, it happened. I lost my job because of it. I am convinced that was why my temporary contract wasn't changed to a permanent position."

We both remained silent for a while. My coffee had gone cold over our conversation and now I was staring at the half-emptied cup, as if the explanation of this puzzle was hiding in there.

"Dr. Swanson, sooner or later the supervisor of that vacant post will hear about this. You know how gossip spreads. What should I do? If I keep this silent it feels like I am betraying my new boss, but if I'm honest about this I might not get the job. I don't know what to do!"

I recognized the dilemma.

"I have to think about this. Right now I'll write to Professor Hanzl and inform him you're interested in this maternity leave replacement. He told me he is going to attend a meeting next week so he'll probably not respond till he comes back. That gives us a bit of time to consider the options."

After a moment I added: "I think I would like to have a word with this Dr. Kazinski first."

She looked horrified.

"Please, Dr. Swanson, don't tell him that I've contacted you. He will take it personally, I know him!" There was panic in her lovely eyes now.

"You can leave that to me. I have my ways to get in touch with him, without mentioning you at all," I smiled. After all, I was writing a book about his research subject, and he would be flattered if I asked his opinion on some matters.

# IV

With the persistence required in such cases I had been able to get past Dr. Kazinski's secretary, and once I had been put through, he was quite friendly and responded positively to my polite request to meet on short notice. He acknowledged he was aware of my scientific performance, although we had never met in person. My collaboration with the forensic lab had finished by the time he became director of the institute, which was less than two years ago. After a brief explanation of the reason of my request, he welcomed the idea of providing expertise for my book from a practical viewpoint. I know how to fawn over a person to get a service in return. We agreed to meet Monday morning.

I had planned a strategy to direct the conversation towards DNA analysis of hair. The forensic literature was divided over the best way to analyse DNA from hair fragments or shed hairs that did not contain the hair root, or follicle. When a hair including its follicle was available, enough nuclear DNA would be present to be amplified by PCR, and this provides an extensive fingerprint. But hair shafts without their follicle contain very little or no nuclear DNA; most of the DNA present in the hair itself is mitochondrial DNA. These are much smaller DNA molecules, so they provide far less information about their owner. I wanted to discuss with Dr. Kazinski how he dealt with the use of mitochondrial DNA markers for one sample, and genomic DNA from another sample, related to the same case. I hoped that would lead the way to discuss the problems with Monica's results.

My daily routine was interrupted by a phone call from a journalist from a local radio station, who requested an interview related to the recent murder. The press had gone in overdrive and now freely talked about a serial killer, carelessly ignoring the difference between speculation and fact. The journalist who contacted me flattered I was a specialist in forensic techniques and he wanted to interview me by telephone, to be broadcasted live, on the use of 'CSI-like methods' (those were his words) to identify a serial killer. I politely declined. I didn't want to become involved in this press theatre; it wasn't even known if the two murders were connected, and I didn't want to step in place of the police press officer, who had undoubtedly been pestered by the same journalist before he came to me.

***

When I knocked on the door of Dr. Gottfried Kazinski's office, I was slightly nervous. I was well aware of the fact that I wanted information from him, and not the other way round. That made my position weaker than his, and I had little room to negotiate. Moreover, I couldn't just walk in and confront him with his lack of professionalism because he had rejected the laboratory results of one assistant and preferred conflicting ones produced by another. Instead, I had to approach the subject indirectly and subtly, which went against my nature. Normally, I like to be frank with people, but this time I couldn't. I hoped to be able to find the right words, without spoiling the opportunity to save the reputation of young Monica Malzberger.

My knock was answered by a voice that was higher than I had expected from a man:

"*Herein bitte!*"

I opened the door and as I started to enter I had to press my lips to avoid a laugh. Did I have to discuss hair with this man? The person who rose from behind his desk was short, with the beginning of a belly, in his mid-thirties, and, to my surprise, he was as bald as a coot. His face was round and round glasses rested on a fleshy nose; the only thing that stopped him from resembling one of Snow White's dwarfs was the lack of a beard.

I composed myself and stepped forward with my hand outstretched, introducing myself:

"Sue Swanson, a pleasure to meet you, sir."

He answered my greeting politely but rather formally and invited me to sit down.

During our conversation I quickly discovered that he compensated his unimpressive physical appearance and his high-pitched voice with a bossy, if not arrogant air. No doubt he had learned to impress the judge with this attitude if he had to; he would frequently have to appear in court to present forensic evidence, and his arrogance would leave little room for uncertainties, so much was obvious. But I saw through his arrogance and I didn't like him. I hoped that was not so obvious. We discussed various methods to extract DNA from hair, the advantages of analysing genomic DNA over mitochondrial DNA, and the difficulties when dealing with samples that contained too little DNA to produce a proper yield. I tried to find a lead to divert the conversation to the three hairs that had caused a personnel change in his team. It was more difficult than I had imagined. Our conversation went on without much progress. I was racking my brains on how to get to my goal as I asked:

"Is a microscopic analysis of hairs that are to be assessed by PCR a standard procedure in your lab?"

He answered with the certainty of someone who is always right.

"Of course it is, but we prefer to do the microscopic examination after, not before the PCR. The first time a sample bag is opened is to take out a sample for PCR. That is the safest way to avoid contamination." I nodded in approval and made some notes in my notebook in order to leave a serious impression.

"And is the same person usually responsible for the PCR and the microscopy?"

"Well, yes. I don't have enough personnel to have two people working on a single sample, do I? Mind, we are a certified lab, and all procedures are performed strictly according to standards, you understand?" He suddenly became offensive, even aggressive, as if my question had suggested I doubted his credentials. Quickly I backed down:

"Yes, yes, no doubt at all. Your lab has an excellent reputation," and tried to steer away from the heat by changing the subject. I mentioned the recent trend to try and predict physical characteristics of an individual based on genetic information obtained from hair. He was sceptical of this, though skin and eye colour could be predicted with a reasonable degree of accuracy, and the geographical origin of the individual could also be roughly mapped. Eventually, when our meeting drew to an end, I could not hold back my true nature and mentioned, more as an afterthought:

"By the way, I happen to know one of your assistants, Frau Monica Malzberger. She is part of your team, isn't she? An excellent lab worker, she used to work in our group. The girl is very good at her job!"

His round face didn't reveal any emotion. The blue eyes behind his round glasses remained cold as he looked directly into mine.

"Frau Malzberger has left, she is no longer working here." No explanation, no response to my comment on her quality of work. What had I expected? He didn't know that I knew why she had left his team.

"Oh, what a shame. A loss to your group, I'm sure. But it is difficult to keep talented workers, isn't it?" I wouldn't let go so easily.

"We found an excellent replacement. I can assure you I hire only the best candidates for my team." It was an indirect insult to Monica. My efforts were useless. This man was as hard as granite. I was unable to penetrate through his shield of arrogance. If I confronted him with my view on his decision, he would not move one millimetre. I gave up.

We finished our conversation and I lied by saying how much I appreciated his help, thanking him painstakingly for his valuable time. With a pride he couldn't conceal he handed me a brochure of his research team, which his PR department had just produced.

"The ink is still wet!" he joked as he gave me the leaflet.

I was glad to get out of his office.

***

Out of frustration I hit the machines in the gym with extra force. The rhythmic movements of my body slowly pacified me. I had tried my best to help Monica; it was all I could have done, and I didn't think the incident that had forced her to leave the Forensic Institute would prevent her from finding another job. *Stop feeling responsible, Sue!*

While I was cycling away the kilometres on the stationary exercise bike as part of my routine training I tried to explain why this thing wouldn't leave my mind. Was it really the future of a young lab assistant that I was concerned about? Or was it because there was an inconsistency in a particular piece of forensic evidence that was blatantly being ignored? The latter, of course. I was frustrated that someone in the position of Gottfried Kazinski allowed himself such sloppiness. That went against everything I believed in: veracity, responsibility, accuracy, reliability. It was for this reason that I couldn't let it go.

In my mind I repeated the facts once more and tried to make sense of them. Monica had received three sample bags, each containing one hair found on the body of a strangled prostitute. Why had these been there in the first place? I didn't know the details of the crime scene, but according to the newspaper the killed woman had been naked, lying on her bed. So presumably this Lena had slept with a client, or had been ready to do so, when she was murdered. There might have been a fight; she might have tried to defend herself against her attacker. Did she pull his hair, and had her fist still clenched the hairs that had been recovered? I played the scene in my head. A prostitute stripping herself, while her customer does the same, probably enjoying the show she performs for him. Once naked, she lays down on her bed, begging him to come closer. He reaches out, his hands caressing the curves of her body, slowly moving up, enjoying her breasts, sliding up to her shoulders, touching her neck... At what point had she noticed something was wrong? Would he have been sitting on top of her while he strangled her? She would have put her hands around his arms, trying to release his grip, kicking with her legs, not being able to remove the weight, panicking as the pressure on her throat increased. Why had he lost hairs during this act of violence? It didn't make sense. But I didn't have enough information about the scene to make a fair judgement.

My mind moved on to the three sample bags. I imagined Monica opening them, one bag after another. She was wearing gloves and her hands worked in a flow cabinet to provide a sterile environment. She cut a bit off one hair and the fragment fell into a tube in which she had already pipetted alcohol. That would rinse the hair and remove any foreign DNA, before the solvent was added to extract the owner's DNA. One tube after another. Three tubes to work with. The procedure of DNA extraction was familiar to me. Monica did it on a daily basis and would not make beginner's mistakes. Three fingerprints had been produced, in an experiment that included a negative control and in which all seemed to be well. She repeated it three times. Three triplicates, all giving the same result. There was no evidence for contamination. Quite the opposite, in fact! If a PCR experiment contains a contaminated ingredient, it typically produces one and the same pattern in all tubes, overwriting the variation that could only have been detected in an uncontaminated experiment. But here, the opposite had happened! Instead of the expected identity of three fingerprints, her experiment had produced three different patterns.

I remembered what Kazinski had said. Monica would have

inspected the remains of the three hairs under the microscope. She had stated, in her report, that the hairs belonged to three individuals. Had she observed microscopic differences between the three hairs? She hadn't told me so, but if the three hairs had looked exactly identical, wouldn't she have doubted her own PCR results?

Next scene. After Kazinski had heard the results, I guess he feared he would be criticized, as his report wouldn't fit the hypothesis of a single *Täter*. Such feedback is against the rules, but the head of investigation would be under a lot of pressure, since this murder case received so much publicity in its early days. Kazinski decided to have the experiment repeated by someone else. What had that second person (Monica had mentioned her name was Gudrun) done different to Monica's procedure, so that her result had been one identical fingerprint pattern obtained from each of the three tubes?

If you want to influence experimental results, it is quite easy. Suppose my chef orders a PCR that should give three identical patterns. I can produce these. But it would be manipulation, *Betrug*, falsification of data. If that's what had happened, and if it were discovered, Kazinski could forget about his certification and his license.

My bike beeped to inform me I had done my twenty minutes. I skipped the cool-down phase. Finished with my workout, I walked towards the showers and nearly bumped into Janine. She was also a regular visitor of our gym, a tall, handsome young woman in her mid-twenties with a beautiful body. Her long chestnut hair was tightened into a roll to the side of her head, which produced an interesting asymmetrical look. She moved in a feline manner, very supple and elegant. More than once I had observed her doing stretching exercises and silently admired her flexibility. I greeted her on my way and she smiled back.

"Are you done already?" We often trained together, when the place was not too crowded and two machines were available next to each other. Now she had only just started while I was sweaty and tired. Her T-shirt looked fresh and she radiated energy. I guess the impression she got of me was the exact opposite. I confirmed that my training was over and could we train together next time, maybe? She smiled again, nodding vaguely, and danced more than walked towards the treadmill.

I showered and watched the foam skid down my legs and slide towards the drain, where it whirled and produced a little white mount, like the cream on top of a pastry. My mind kept asking the same questions. How did one murderer leave three hairs on the body of his victim? Or, in case there had been three instead of one offender, why had each of them left a single hair?

# V

Back home I emptied my sports bag to put the sweaty garments in the laundry. Loading the washing machine, a faint and unfamiliar scent filled my nose. Something sweet and pleasant, but what was it? Curiously I removed the laundry from the drum again, and sniffed at my T-shirt, my shorts, the towel I had used, even my socks. It wasn't any of those. It was one of Robert's shirts, the one he had worn yesterday. It smelled faintly of a female perfume, a brand that I didn't use. *Damn!*

Crossed, I closed the door of the washing machine with so much force that it bounced open again. He had come home late last night, as usual. Without an explanation. Perfume. Those phone calls. *I'm not stupid, you know!* I felt my anger grow. Feelings of hurt, jealousy and hate fought for dominance. The idiot! The bastard! How could he!

As I grabbed my sports bag to take it out of the laundry room, the brochure fell out that Kazinski had handed me that afternoon – I remembered I had slipped it in that bag when I got inside my car. Now I crumbled it with disgust, as if that piece of paper symbolized the wrongdoings of my husband. I would tell him what I thought of his betrayal! I would make it clear that I couldn't accept this! I would, I would… I collapsed in a chair, sobbing, the silly brochure still clenched in my fist.

Eventually I calmed down a bit. *Think before you act, Sue.* There was a lot to lose if I risked my marriage. Robert was the father of my two sons; we were a family whose members respected each other. Did I want to disrupt the harmony, take Robert away from his boys, destroy his ego in the eyes of his sons? And there was the house, which we owned together; most of our savings were invested in the property. In case we split up, we would have to sell. I was financially independent (at least, most of the time), but I didn't want to start all over; the life of a divorced-woman-over-fifty didn't appeal. Robert was not a bad husband to live with; we had been together long enough to naturally complement each other. He provided mental support when I needed it, and I guided him in some of his professional decisions. We had experienced good times and bad times, like in every marriage. I liked his sense of humour, and we normally got on well together. We knew each other so well that we hardly ever had a row; we knew each other's weak sides and avoided these if we could, or otherwise accepted them. Our lives were intermingled in so many ways it would be difficult to separate. I didn't want a separation, let alone a divorce, but I expected loyalty from my husband!

Absentmindedly, I opened the crumbled paper that was still in my fist and started to smoothen the cracks. A photograph at the back of the brochure showed the research team of Kazinski's institute. The whole team presented itself in front of the entrance of the building, smiling into the camera. It had to be a recent photo: Monica was not amongst them.

I went to the kitchen to make myself a cup of tea. I was not going to confront Robert with my discovery tonight. Not yet. I would observe him closely, and check his whereabouts if I could, without letting him know that I was keeping an eye on him. Spying on my husband? No, just keeping my eyes open, that was all.

With my cup of tea in front of me I looked at the photograph again. I wondered if Gudrun was on the photo. Who, of the fifteen women shown, would she be? I wasn't yet going to throw this brochure away.

***

I needed to talk to someone, to focus my thoughts. I was still too upset to go back to my writing. I had imagined how it would be to be divorced, and although it wasn't an attractive future, I had decided to keep all options open. In order to be prepared, I called my dear friend, Peter Eichholz. He had helped me out on a few occasions when I needed legal advice, though, fortunately, I had never officially needed his service as a lawyer. At least, up till now. He worked in a *Kanzlei*, a law firm specialized in the defence of criminal charges. He would also know about divorces, or else he could recommend me someone. I hadn't talked to him for a long time.

Peter was surprised to hear from me. He was on the road when I called; I recognized the sound of a car's engine in the background.

"Hi Sue! Well, that has been a long time… everything all right with you?"

That must be a standard phrase for a lawyer. Most people would call him when everything was not right.

"Yeah, don't worry. I wanted to have a word with you, when you have the time. Can I call you back later?"

We agreed that he would call me back in about an hour. It gave me time to recover from my shock.

By the time Peter rang back, I had made up my mind that I would not mention Robert. I didn't want to go that route, not yet, at least. Nevertheless, it was good to talk to Peter. We had known each other for a long time. I had met him at a scientific meeting, where he had presented a lecture about the legal responsibility of the medical profession, his specialization at that time. We had become friends, and over the years had remained in touch (he had written me emails more often than I had contacted him, but I had nearly always replied to his mails). He had changed directions and now worked in the field that was actually in line with the subject of my book. So when he asked what I was doing lately, I mentioned my latest project. He could suffice as a typical reader, someone who would profit from the contents. I asked how much experience he had with forensic evidence. It turned out he had had his share.

"The most difficult thing for me is the statistics. I always get confused with those numbers and chances and odds. I've never been very good at maths. If you could explain that in a way that we, simple lawyers with a small brain, can understand it, that would be great!" he joked. I promised I would do my best, and asked if he would be willing to read through a few chapters in the near future. He said he'd be happy to do so, and he wouldn't charge his time! *Good old Peter.* Listening to his warm voice made me feel better. He would never know what my original intention had been to call him.

I put down the telephone and stared at my desk. Then I took up the phone again. There were a few things I needed to know.

"Hi Monica, it's me, Sue Swanson."

***

I was waiting in my car outside the building of the Forensic Institute. It was nearly five p.m., and people were leaving the building after a day's work. Memories of the past floated by, of the years that I had spent three days a week working here. Those had been good years for me, when the boys were still young, and my work had led to a couple of successes, and Robert and I had still been happy… Compare that with my current situation and I could become depressed again! I realized I wasn't far off that route. I had spent three days cleaning my house, starting with the kitchen, as my state of mind had not been fit for scientific writing. Cleaning the house had always been a good therapy when I had been troubled by something. You set yourself a task that is urgently needed anyway and you get instant gratification for your work, as it is obvious what you've accomplished. Moreover, by cleaning up and bringing order into your surroundings, your mind clears as well. At least, that had worked for me in the past. This time was slightly different. My troubles didn't go away by polishing woodwork, emptying cupboards and removing cobwebs. But the acute pain of my discovery was subdued and I was able to think clearly again. Robert had been home early every night, apart from Wednesday, when he said he had to see Tom. This was the son of a friend of ours, a whiz kid who looked after our computers. Robert said there was a problem with his laptop, and when he left indeed had taken his computer with him. When I called Tom two hours later, pretending I needed to ask Robert something, he stated Robert had just left. Since he turned up twenty minutes later (about the time that was needed to drive from Tom's place back home) that could not be called suspicious. Robert behaved normally, and I didn't know what to think.

This afternoon I decided to check something that had been on my mind whenever I wasn't thinking about my marriage.

When I had asked Monica what Gudrun looked like, she had described her as a thin woman, mid-thirties, who dyed her short hair a brutal red. With that description it had been easy to identify her in the team photograph. Her face was thin, with a sharp nose and small eyes. Her hair was indeed brightly coloured, and she wore it as if she was coming straight out of bed, though I knew it required careful styling, with a lot of gel, to make it look like that. The fact that she was shown in that photograph had made me wonder, because Monica had told me that Gudrun had been on a temporary contract, which had been about to expire when the mishap took place.

Waiting in my car I was now watching the building to check if Gudrun was still working here. If so, I might even have a word with her, though I hadn't made up my mind whether that would be a good thing to do. I had been waiting here since four o'clock, listening to a CD of Beethoven's ninth, a 1996 recording of Herbert von Karajan conducting the *Berliner Philharmoniker*. The last part, with the choir singing Schiller's *'Ode an die Freude'* was nearly finished when I spotted Gudrun as she was leaving the building. With the colour of her hair it was easy to identify her. I lowered the volume of the music and watched her as she turned to the left, towards the low extension where (according to the sign) bicycles could be parked. I hesitated. Should I follow her, and talk to her before she had mounted her bike to ride home? The main purpose of my watch had been fulfilled. I now knew she still worked in Kazinski's lab. Either her temporary contract had been extended, or, which I thought more likely, she had been given the permanent position that Monica had hoped for. I decided to wait, but strangely enough, she didn't emerge from the bicycle parking. The music had finished. I waited. Then I saw Gottfried Kazinski leaving the main building, with his car keys dangling from his hand, but instead of turning right in the direction of the car park, he turned left towards the bicycle building and entered it. When neither of them reappeared, I left my car and approached the extension that had now swallowed them both. I tiptoed to the entrance, where steps led down approximately two metres below street level, with a ramp on both sides of the stairs to lead a bicycle in and out. Halfway down I peeked inside. Rows and rows of bicycle racks, most of them empty now. Then I saw two people at the back of the badly lit room, in a tight embrace. They were oblivious of the world around them.

I returned to my car and drove home. I had seen enough.

# VI

"I know it sounds crazy but I believe that is what happened!"

We were sitting at my kitchen table, a mug of green tea in front of us. I had asked her to come over because we had things to discuss. Professor Hanzl had responded positively after he got back from his travels and had asked for an official application letter. I had told Monica we needed to meet because of the letter of recommendation that I was going to write. Now I had told her of my suspicion that Gudrun had deliberately falsified the outcome of the PCR she had repeated when Monica's results didn't suit their boss.

Monica didn't want to believe it. She had never liked Gudrun, she said, but couldn't imagine someone would corrupt an experimental outcome. I decided it would be better not to mention the love affair. All I said was: "Look, I've got a feeling they've played behind your back. Both you and Gudrun were on a temporary contract that was running out, and it seems it was only possible to keep one of you permanently. I believe, for reasons I won't elaborate on, that your boss wanted to keep Gudrun in his group. Then you produced results that put Kazinski in a vulnerable position, as it opposed the working hypothesis of the police. So he decided it favourable to present the results he presumed they wanted, and asked Gudrun to produce them. That provided him with a reason to get rid of you. In return for her cooperation he offered her the permanent position. Doesn't that sound plausible?" *And in this way he ensured his sweetheart would remain in his vicinity,* I added in my thoughts.

"Dr. Swanson, *mit Verlaub*, it sounds crooked. Who would do that? I mean, Dr. Kazinski risks his reputation, and how would Gudrun be able to produce the results he wanted?" Dear Monica, she was such an honest girl! She wouldn't even consider results could be faked.

"He probably told her what the outcome of the PCR should be, and since she urgently needed a permanent position, she produced whatever he wanted. To some people that's worth a little fake experiment."

"But this is forensic evidence!" Monica exclaimed. She would never lower herself to the level of fallacy.

"I know," I said softly, and remained silent for a while.

I reconsidered the other piece of information Monica had given me by telephone last time we had spoken, and which she had confirmed this afternoon: based on her microscopic observations the three hairs could have been from different individuals. Although their diameter had shown a variance within the acceptable range, and their colour was the same (black), at five hundred times magnitude she had noticed differences in the structure of the cuticle, the 'scales' that build the outside of a hair shaft. This could mean the hairs had grown at different rates, which is unlikely if they had grown on the same scalp. However, that observation alone was not convincing evidence. It just supported her conclusion that these hairs came from three individuals. I continued thinking aloud, in an attempt to acknowledge there were gaps in my hypothesis:

"All right, we can't be certain that this is what has happened. If only we could repeat that PCR, I'd love to do it myself..." Monica looked at me in disbelief.

"That's impossible!"

But it wasn't. It was difficult, but not impossible. A plan developed in my mind, which could once and for all produce the truth about the three hairs. It was not without risks, and I needed Monica's help; that was the difficult bit. She was strongly against it.

We talked for a long time, or rather, I did most of the talking, trying to convince her that we should do this together. She kept opposing me. I needed her because she had access to the forensic lab, and knew where the samples were being stored. It took me all the persuasion I could produce to talk her into this. Eventually she gave in. But before we could put our plan into practice, she would have to get the job in Professor Hanzl's group. So we sat down at my computer and I composed a letter of recommendation, after which I helped her draft the application letter. I suggested she mention 'personal reasons' in case she was asked why she had left her last job. That was sufficiently vague and private to stop most job interviewers from probing further, and would explain why she did not provide a *Zeugnis*, a letter of recommendation, from her last boss. I promised her to call Hanzl personally to convince him of her qualities. I was certain that he would take her on board. Whether Monica would cooperate with the rest of my plan, I was less certain about. I just hoped she wouldn't get too scared before the time came to put our plan into practice.

***

More than a week had passed, and the weather had changed. The last snow had been washed away by three days of continuous rain, and now it was extremely mild for the time of the year. Male blackbirds were busy chasing each other, competing for the best females, and tomtits were seesawing their monotonous calls in the trees as if spring had already arrived, although it was still February. Monica had been offered the job in Hanzl's lab, as I had expected, and right now she was paying a visit to her former colleagues. It had been part of the plan for today; a plan that we had carefully prepared. Two days ago Monica had called her best lab mate in Kazinski's group and subtly hinted that she would like to come over around teatime, as she had some news to announce. Of course she had been most welcome (she had been as popular in this group as she had been in mine) and the arrangement was made for today. Around three she had entered the building of the Forensic Institute with a visitor's pass, which she had collected at the reception. I had given her a lift to her former work place.

We had talked this through in great detail. Monica had confirmed what I thought I had seen the day I had discovered the lovers: there was an emergency exit from the main building leading directly into the bicycle park extension. With this knowledge I had inspected the place once more, taking a closer look at the bicycle park house, which was open to the street. My inspection revealed that there was no CCTV in there (maybe that was why the lovers had chosen this location to kiss and cuddle). When nobody was around I had taken a photo of the emergency exit door and had shown it to our neighbour down the road, *Herr* Stein, a locksmith close to retirement. He confirmed that this door lacked an electronic security system. (I had told him this was a piece of evidence for my niece, who was involved in a burglary claim with an insurance company. It was a lousy story but he grinned in a conspiratorial manner and didn't ask any questions.) My neighbour explained such doors were standard emergency exits; they had a press-down bar that opened the door from the inside, but they could not be opened from the outside. ("Unless you use brute force!" he had added with that grin. Only after we had parted did I remember our front door lock, which I had wanted to ask him about as well.)

Now I was waiting in my car, which I had parked on the side of the street, a little distance away from the car park. I waited to pick Monica up, hoping she was OK; she had been nervous about our adventure. When she came out of the main entrance, she quickly walked towards my car; in fact, she nearly ran the distance. Slightly out of breath, she jumped inside.

"Done it! I can't believe what I've just done, but I've done it!" She inhaled deeply, then rambled on: "Anyway, the colleagues were glad to see me, and they congratulated me over my new job. Fortunately I didn't run into Dr. Kazinski, and Gudrun doesn't work on Fridays. It was actually quite nice to be back there."

She continued to tell me about her former colleagues nonstop, as if by constant talking her nerves would calm down. Eventually she confirmed what I had suspected: Gudrun had been given the post she had expected to be offered herself.

"See, all evidence suggests there was a hidden agenda behind your boss's actions. I'm convinced we are on to something." She watched me and a frown showed on her forehead as she admitted:

"Dr. Swanson, I am frightened about this... we shouldn't continue, really! We can still stop here. No harm's been done yet."

"Don't worry, we'll be fine. I'll drive you home now, and will pick you up at eleven, as we've arranged. OK?"

After that, she remained silent during the rest of the drive.

***

The car park of the Forensic Institute was empty and dark. It was nearly half past eleven. I had parked my car at the same spot I had used seven hours before. That afternoon, when Monica had been inside the building, she had opened the emergency door that led to the bicycle park house, and left it ajar with a small stone placed inside to stop it from closing. On its inner side, the door opened to a corridor that was a dead end, and few people passed there. Chances were that nobody would have noticed the door wasn't properly locked.

We walked our way from the car to the bicycle park house,

slightly hunching and fighting against an urge to run. The Institute was deserted and the only light visible from the outside of the building was the emergency illumination of the staircases that glowed a faint greenish light through the windows. There was no night guide, but that didn't stop me from feeling uncomfortable. I knew Monica was frankly scared.

There were three bicycles parked in the extension at this late hour. Two had a flat tire and one had a broken chain. At the back of the building the emergency door was indeed open, barely noticeable from this side. It provided us entrance to the main building without difficulty. I kicked the stone away and closed the door behind us. The corridor on the inside of the emergency exit was dark, so the torches that I had brought turned out to be useful. Monica led the way. Up two flights of stairs we went, through another dark corridor, until Monica opened the door of a cold room, a walk-in refrigerator where large amounts of materials and fluids were stored that required constant cooling. From a box she took a key that opened the door of 'her' laboratory. The humming sound of fridges and freezers welcomed us and I recognized the typical laboratory smell, a mix of various chemicals, solutes and ozone that the sterilizing UV lamps produced during the night. We didn't switch on the main lights and moved by the light of our torches and the eerie UV of the laminar flow cabinets. After we had taken our coats off, Monica, who knew where the samples were stored, whispered:

"Shall I get them?" I smiled and replied, in a normal voice:

"There is no reason to whisper. We're all on our own. Yes, let's get started. I'll fetch you some ice. Is the ice machine still in the same place?" It had been a long time since I had been in this building. I grabbed an ice bucket and went in the direction Monica pointed at to collect crushed ice, required to cool the precious DNA and all those chemicals that are not stable at room temperature.

When I was back in the lab Monica was wearing the lab coat she had brought. Now she switched on the laminar flow cabinet; its inside changed from UV to normal lighting and a fan started up with an incredible noise.

"Isn't it surprising how noisy those machines are? And you only notice it when you're on your own!" I remarked. Monica nodded, her face now glowing in the light of the flow cabinet. We had worked late nights together in the past, and I recalled the feeling when a lab is slowly emptying until all colleagues are gone.

Somehow you don't notice how the voices and footsteps die away as the others are leaving until suddenly you're all on your own and realize how quiet it is around you. It is spookier to enter an empty lab at night. It is outright scary when you break into a lab that you are not allowed to enter at all.

Monica had collected the sample bags containing the hairs from the freezer. She showed me the labels on the bags. We had decided to repeat both the DNA extraction and the PCR reaction, just to be certain we reproduced every step. When she had left her job, all her notes had to stay in the laboratory, and these were now locked away in the documentary room that we had no access to, but it didn't matter: she knew the codes of the sample bags by heart, and their location in the freezer hadn't changed. In fact, she knew the whole procedure from memory. Nevertheless, she had written out every step, in neat handwriting, on a piece of paper so that I could tick away every step she performed.

Without a word, she put on sterile gloves and started working. She wrote a number on each of three sterile tubes and put them in a rack. I noticed her hands were trembling when she opened the first sample bag to take out its hair using sterile pincers, but by the time she had cut a fragment from the third hair her hands were calmly performing their routine tasks. She worked meticulously and concentrated and seemed to have forgotten that I was present, watching her, checking and ticking off everything she did.

The table centrifuge produced an extremely loud noise, which was completely normal; you just don't notice it so much during the day. Ten minutes we had to wait.

"Is there anything I can do for the next step?" I had to raise my voice over the noise. But she didn't want me to assist. This was her act of honour.

When the DNA extraction was completed, Monica used a precision pipette to put five microlitres of each DNA solution into tubes that were so tiny they disappeared between her gloved fingers. It was time for part two of tonight's endeavour: the PCR reaction. For this we had to go to another lab, a room where isolated DNA was strictly forbidden, to avoid contamination. Monica changed into a clean lab coat and handed me one as well. I would not have thought about bringing lab coats, but she had thoroughly prepared herself. The room she led me to was small and didn't have a window; it only contained a freezer where the components were stored for DNA amplification, and a bench to work on. A flask of alcohol stood ready to clean the work place. Lab workers would only spend a short time here to prepare their PCR vials; the room was exclusively used for that purpose. Monica took a few vials out of the freezer and thawed their contents between her fingers, tapping them to check that all ice inside had gone, then she put them in the ice bucket. She next produced the 'master mix', the solution that contained all components required for the PCR, other than DNA. She pipetted, in one larger tube that she put back in the ice bucket after every act, the buffer, nucleotides, primers and the required amount of sterile water. She had done this a thousand times. Always with full concentration, always with utmost precision. Now she added a minute amount of DNA polymerase, the expensive enzyme that would knit the nucleotides into strands of DNA, copies of the genetic material that belonged to the person on whose head the hair had once grown that we were examining. The master mix was ready. Monica cleaned up, put all components back in the freezer, wiped the workplace with alcohol, and then we brought the ice bucket with the master mix back to the lab.

Once the five tiny tubes (one negative control, one positive control and the three hair samples) had received their portion of the master mix, they were put in the PCR machine. The tubes stood there like little soldiers in a rank. The lid of the machine was closed, Monica pressed the buttons to select the correct programme, and pressed 'start'. All the machine needed to do was to heat and cool the tubes at required temperatures for defined periods of time, one round after another, to allow the enzyme to do its work. It would take two hours to complete. She sighed and moved her shoulders in an attempt to relax.

"Well done!" I said in encouragement. It sounded silly. This had been her daily routine. It was nearly an insult to complement her with this.

"I could do with a cup of coffee," she replied with a weak voice. Her bag contained a thermos flask and two cups. The girl had thought about everything!

# VII

Somehow, I had known what the result of this PCR would be. Still, when I saw the patterns on the monitor of the computer that was connected to the electrophoresis equipment, I felt my heartbeat increase. The positive control showed up strong and neat as expected; the lane of the negative control remained empty. The three DNA samples produced multiple peaks that represented DNA bands of various lengths. I compared the three patterns by sight; they were all different. We had opted for the mitochondrial DNA PCR, since the roots of the hairs were no longer available. It didn't matter this test produced less information than a nuclear DNA test. The outcome was one hundred percent certain.

I took a photograph of the screen with my smartphone, after which Monica deleted the file from the computer that had visualized the bands. She cleaned up all our traces in a routine manner without making a fuzz, but tonight had brought significant progress. The girl had reproduced her results, for the fourth time now, with an independent DNA isolation and a different PCR test, and I had been her witness. There was no doubt that those three hairs, which had been collected from the body of a murdered woman, belonged to three different individuals. No doubt at all.

***

By the time I got in bed, it was nearly dawn. I was wide awake, listening to the soft snoring of Robert, who had not woken up when I slipped in, while the events of tonight played merry-go-round in my head. My main motivation for this action had been to get confirmation, to understand what had caused the unexplainable differences in PCR results, but now I wasn't sure about my next move. My first thought had been to inform the police. But on second thought, that wasn't a smart thing to do: if I presented my discovery to the police, I could be arrested for *Hausfriedensbruch*, breaking into private property. As well as tampering with forensic evidence, and God knows what other offences they could charge me with. I would most likely need the help of my friend Peter the lawyer to get me out of the mess I would bring myself into, if he could help me at all. It would be very unwise to report my findings to the police.

On the other hand, tonight's efforts had clearly shown that the forensic report that Kazinski had produced based on Gudrun's work was wrong. The chief inspector who had received that report couldn't know the data were false, unless I informed him of my findings, so he might be on the wrong track with his investigations as a result of the manipulations.

Robert turned to his other side and groaned; he was waking up. Saturday morning was his time for sports. He had recently taken up running, which I had encouraged, to fight the pounds. In about an hour he would meet with a group of friends for two hours of intensive training. While he was in the bathroom I got up, slightly dizzy from lack of sleep, and started preparing coffee for two. No questions were asked about last night, and I didn't volunteer to tell him of my whereabouts. We had breakfast in silence.

When he was gone I switched on my computer and searched the Internet to find out who was in charge of the investigations of the last two murder cases. Disappointingly, the name of the chief inspector wasn't made public. The police had posted a public statement that the two murders were considered unrelated and that the investigations were ongoing. A suspect had not yet been identified for either case. Help from the public was appreciated, and a telephone number was available in case someone could provide further information. I wrote the number down, thinking it could wait till Monday to decide whether I would call.

I used this Saturday to go on my first bicycle ride of this year, now that the snow was gone and the weather was so mild. It was good to feel the wind in my face, so much better than being on an indoor exercise bike! The earth smelled of spring, and the cornel bushes were flowering. If the weather stayed like this, the forsythia bushes would soon be in bloom, too. Close to the river, celandine flowers had appeared like little yellow stars. While I passed them I wondered why most spring flowers were yellow – did that have something to do with the preference of early insects? I would have to look this up some time. I tried not to think about work, to close my mind to my book, PCR fingerprints or forensic evidence.

Instead, I let my legs do the work and concentrated on my breathing. The drowsiness of the sleepless night left me, and by the time I came back, I felt refreshed and energetic. I was fit enough to spend the rest of the weekend on my writing.

***

Of course I called the police; my conscience wouldn't allow otherwise. Monday morning I dialled the number I had copied from the Internet and asked if I could speak to the head of investigations.

"*Worum geht es*?" asked the female police officer with an uninterested voice on the other end. She would not put me through, just like that, without knowing if I was a serious caller. The police received a lot of sham calls whenever they opened a special number related to a criminal case.

"I have information related to the murder of Lena Lotus; information that is confidential and important for the investigations. I will only share it with the chief inspector in person and I require protection of my source; I am prepared to pay a visit to the police station to discuss my conditions."

"Just a moment, please." The police woman was probably impressed about my decisive and professional tone – at least, I liked to believe so, and that I had been convincing enough to be put through to the officer in charge.

I listened to a silly melody while she connected my call.

"Braun," said a male voice in a demanding tone when my connection came through.

"Good morning, this is Sue Swanson speaking. Have I been connected to the officer responsible for the prostitute murder cases?"

"*Hauptkommissar* Braun. What can I do for you?" The tone was not particularly friendly. But hang on, I knew this voice! And that name... Braun... which Braun did I know? It took a moment before my brain took the right turn.

"*Ehm*, is this Herr Steffan Braun, the father of Melanie? I'm Andrew Callighan's mother!" It is confusing to Germans that I use a different name than my children, who bear Robert's family name. If this officer Braun was the person I thought he was, his daughter had been to school with my youngest son.

"Ah, yes, I remember, the English family! What can I do for you, Mrs Calli… Mrs Swanson?" he repeated his question more friendly now.

This could turn out to be easier than I had feared. I remembered Herr Braun as a sympathetic person, reasonable and intelligent.

"I have information that I believe is highly relevant to your investigations, Herr Braun. Maybe we can arrange a visit?"

He suggested to meet on Wednesday morning in his office, ten o'clock. I felt relieved when I put the phone down.

***

"*Die Sache ist delikat.*" Delicate is what you could call this! I was sitting in the office of Chief Inspector Steffan Braun. He hadn't changed much since I had last seen him, other than that his hair had turned quite grey now. He was a handsome man, tall, broad shoulders, square chin. The kind of man a woman feels protected by. His brown eyes were sharp and the bushy eyebrows looked friendlier now that they had changed from black to grey. I particularly remembered his common sense; we had both attended a number of long, seemingly everlasting parent assembly evenings where discussions about subjects that I considered completely irrelevant would go on and on, never reaching an agreement in lack of a skilled chairperson. Then, at some point, Herr Braun would make a well-formulated remark that miraculously turned all arguments into one direction. I admired the way he could, politely and determined at the same time, make people agree on something that they had only a minute ago vehemently disagreed on. I also remembered him as a dedicated father. How proud he had been when his daughter Melanie had played a piano piece at the school concert. Steffan Braun was a sensible man, and I hoped he would accept what I had to offer him without asking too many questions.

After a handshake we exchanged the obligatory civilities. I informed him of my writing project, to introduce him to my profession (he hadn't known I was knowledgeable about forensics as my husband and I had both rather vaguely introduced ourselves as 'scientists' at school gatherings, without giving details to other parents about our exact professions). For this occasion I was wearing a suit, which I considered made me look more professional. Now I had to come to my point. I had to tell him what I knew, and how I knew it.

He listened in silence. He didn't ask questions, didn't take notes, he just sat there and listened. The news that Kazinski had rejected lab results at his own account didn't seem to upset him. He probably relied on the judgement of his experts, but he would not show disapproval when he discovered such judgement could be questioned. When I described our nightly adventure, he briefly frowned, but didn't interrupt. He let me tell the complete story, at my own pace, until I was done.

"So, if I may ask, you have witnessed how those three hair samples were analysed, and from the results you're suggesting they belong to three individuals, in contrast to what the official forensic report states." It was a conclusion, not a question.

"Not just suggesting, the evidence is overwhelming. There is no doubt at all that there are three individuals, not one, whose hair was analysed. I've taken a photo of the computer screen showing the fingerprints. Have a look!" He bent over to peek at the screen of my smartphone. I could smell his aftershave.

"I see." I wasn't sure, though, if he understood what he was looking at. If only my book had been finished!

There was a pause.

"You do realize we can't use your information in our investigations, and that your observations would not hold in court." It was a neutral statement, not presented as criticism.

"I know, but that doesn't make the information less relevant to your case."

"Correct, but more difficult to implement in our investigations." He had never needed many words to make his point.

Another pause.

"I see no other option than to formally accept the data presented in the forensic report, in other words, to officially assume a single culprit, but with the knowledge that you've disclosed we have to face the possibility there were actually three persons present at the crime scene. It will be difficult to incorporate this knowledge in our working hypothesis, but I thank you for informing me."

He cleared his throat and said, with the typical intonation of a conversation drawing to an end:

"Mrs Swanson, I must..."

"Call me Sue," I interrupted, but he didn't rephrase his sentence, nor did he get the joke.

"... thank you for your time, and ask you to remain available for further information in which case we will contact you. That is the official procedure." With a sudden change in his voice he added, less formal and friendlier now:

"However, I wouldn't want to miss the chance to discuss a difficult case like this with an expert in forensic methods." I accepted the complement with a nod.

"In order to keep to the procedures, I suggest we end our conversation here and now. I would, however, appreciate if you called this telephone number some time after work hours this week, so that we can discuss further developments at a different location." He handed me his card, on the back of which he had written his private telephone number. He looked at me in earnest.

"And I insist all our discussions remain strictly confidential."

"Certainly!" I couldn't agree more, on my part. After all, I had just admitted to a police officer that I'd broken in a certified laboratory and tampered with forensic evidence. These things should rather remain confidential! I promised to contact him soon, and left in good spirits.

***

Back home I checked my email and discovered a message from my publisher. They politely enquired when they could receive a first draft of a book chapter, which they wanted to review in case I needed to adjust style or content. It didn't have to be chapter one, they just wanted to see a sample chapter in draft form. I wrote a reply that I needed a bit more time, since it had only been a few weeks since we had signed the contract, while in my mind I promised myself to concentrate on my writing now, or the book would never be done. The only other thing that I had to do before turning to its contents was to call Monica, and ensure her that everything was all right. I did that straight away and told her I had contacted the police, and that I had been assured our information would be handled in confidence. I swore to her I had not disclosed her name. She had nothing to fear, and I wished her luck on her new job, which was to start on the first of March, in a few days from now. Then I concentrated on my chapters.

## VIII

"I would like to hear your view on this case. So far we had assumed we dealt with one suspect, but now it appears we have three possible suspects. I find that hard to accept, to be quite honest with you." We were seated next to each other on a comfortable couch in a lounge room; on the low glass table in front of us were two glasses of wine. He had suggested to meet here, when I had called him at home on Thursday night to arrange an appointment. The place had a futuristic look, with lamps resembling UFOs – they didn't produce much light but were of an interesting design. There was music in the background, something Latin American, pleasant and not too loud. Couches were placed so that groups of four to eight people could share a private cubicle, and these were separated by wooden screens. The cubicles left and right from us were empty. Nevertheless, we kept our voices down.

Steffan Braun had exactly phrased the concerns I had felt about our findings. It didn't make sense that there would be three suspects involved in the strangling of a single prostitute. He had agreed to share protected information with me in confidence, in return for picking my brain.

"I don't have to point out to you that the presence of a stain at a crime scene is not sufficient evidence to assume guilt. Those hairs could have been left by previous customers," I tried.

He shook his head.

"Those hairs were recovered from the body of the victim. I was there when *Spusi* secured them." *Spusi* was short for *Spurensicherheit*, the crime scene investigators who would have crawled over the victim and her surroundings wearing gloves and protective overalls, in search of traces of the murderer.

I digested this new information while I sipped from my wine.

"Isn't it strange that those hairs were found on the body in the first place? I mean, let's assume there were three men present during the crime, why would each of them lose a hair, a single hair, and leave it on the body? What about other stains?"

"Negative. There were no skin remains under her fingernails, no semen, no saliva. And so many smeared fingerprints in the apartment that they are useless. We found traces of latex on her skin, so we assume the suspect, or suspects, I should now say, wore latex. Could be a fetishism."

We were both silent for a moment, trying to imagine a scenario that would fit these facts. A foursome of three men and a woman, all men wearing latex while she was naked – it seemed ridiculous to me.

"There is something else I would like to mention. I guess you've heard of the second murder? Again the victim was a prostitute, and she seemed well-to-do. Luxury apartment, expensive furniture, you get the picture. She was found strangled on her bed, like the first case. This time we found two hairs, which are currently being analysed. Yes, in Kazinski's lab. But the hairs are blond, while those first three were black. So we had assumed there was no connection between the two cases." I remembered that had been the official statement made public.

"Now I'm not so sure there is no connection," I nodded.

"I know this is speculation, but we have to anticipate that if those two blond hairs are also from two different individuals, Kazinski might not put that in his report. I would recommend you have those samples analysed somewhere else."

Again he shook his head; it would be difficult to change laboratory services without a valid reason.

"OK, so let's assume the two hairs will again result in different DNA fingerprints, whether reported to you as such or not. It would mean we are dealing with five suspects, which is just silly. It could be, I mean, it is likely, even, that those hairs do not belong to the killer or killers at all."

I recalled a case of DNA evidence that stirred up Germany a few years ago. It started with a murder case where a DNA sample found a match in the database. Two things were unusual about it. First of all, the DNA belonged to a woman, while the majority of crimes, including murder, are committed by men. Second, the match was found to a DNA stain involved in a minor crime. Over the months and years, the DNA of this female killer (the media dubbed her the *Phantom Killerin*, the 'ghost she-killer') turned up, in various kinds of crimes, from various locations. One time her DNA was found in France. Another time, the whole of Germany was shocked when a policewoman was brutally killed after she had stopped a car for a routine road control. In all these cases, DNA of the *Phantom Killerin* had been detected. How could someone be involved in minor burglaries as well as in homicide, be active over a period of years, all over the country and even in France, kill several people including a police officer, and be so sloppy to leave her DNA behind wherever she went? The riddle took years to be solved. Eventually, it was discovered that the DNA came from the cotton swabs that the *Spusi* had used to take samples. It belonged to the woman who had packed the swabs in the factory. She could not be held responsible: although those swabs were sold sterile (after packing they had been sterilized by UV irradiation) they were not guaranteed to be DNA-free. They had never been suitable for forensic applications, and were not offered as such, but they were cheaper than the swabs sold for this purpose. Obviously, the person who had bought the cheaper alternative to be used by forensic investigators didn't know about the power of PCR.

I thought it better not to mention that horror case to Steffan – the German police had been the international laughingstock. Besides, that sort of contamination caused matches in DNA fingerprints, while here we were dealing with the opposite: DNA fingerprints belonging to different individuals although they should have been from one suspect only.

Steffan had finished his glass and ordered another round. I resumed:

"Here are the facts: three black hairs from different individuals were found on the body of a victim where one killer is most likely. Two blond hairs were found on a second body. There are significant similarities between the two murders. So is there a relation between the two? With what had the women been strangled?"

"The first one with her bra. The second one we are not certain, but the pressure marks on her neck suggest he used his hands." I noticed Braun would not use the names of the victims. Possibly it would be easier for him to detach his emotions if the victims were just that, victims, bodies, not a person with a name and a life. I evaluated the details about the strangling method.

"You know what is maddening? If those hairs had not been found, I would have said these are two independent cases. Especially with this difference in strangulation method. The second might've been a copycat murder, but the copycat didn't know about the bra, as that information had not been released to the public. But because of those hairs, we think there is a connection. I say, *we think*, as the human mind is very keen on identifying connections, even if there are none. Because on both victims hairs were found, which in itself is rather atypical, we see a connection. And yet, it is those hairs that destroy the working hypothesis of a common suspect, as they do not belong to the same individual. Not within the single case and not between the cases. So why do those different hairs connect the two?" I had been thinking aloud and I wasn't certain Steffan could follow my way of reasoning. He waited for me to continue, not revealing what he was thinking. So I just went on with my line of thoughts:

"Could it be they have been placed at the crime scene on purpose? Where on the body were they found, if I may ask?"

Steffan couldn't remember exactly for the first case and wouldn't tell me for the second. He insisted on checking in the dossier and calling me at lunchtime tomorrow. He was careful not to be caught in the office disclosing protected information to me.

We had exhausted our brains; it was time to relax. He stretched his legs under the glass table and his arms above his head. Then he spread his arms out and laid them on the back of the couch, his right arm behind my head, totally at ease. He was able to disconnect himself from work in a second; I guess one has to have that ability in order to survive in a job like his. I was extremely aware of that arm, so close to my neck. If I leaned back slightly, I would touch it, and his posture would no longer be innocent. Instead of leaning backward, I bent forward to pick up my glass. We toasted to a rapid solution of these cases and to the success of our secret collaboration. While I looked at him over our clunking glasses, I couldn't help thinking what a handsome man he was.

***

Higher and higher I climbed. My legs were tired, my breathing was fast and my heart raced. Sweat trickled down my back. I couldn't last much longer; my legs would soon start to hurt. I checked the display: two minutes left. *Keep going, Sue, only two minutes!* I straightened my back and concentrated on my breathing. The machine next to me moved at an even higher pace. Finally, a beep released me from my torture. I had finished my exercise. I climbed down from the stepper and tried to catch my breath, while

Janine was still going strong on her stepper. She was in a better condition than I was, and usually used a few more pounds on the weights of the machines that we used during our workout. Given that she was more than twenty years younger than me, I felt no inclination to keep up with her. Despite our difference in levels, we enjoyed training together. She was close to finishing while I programmed the treadmill on the right for a five-minute cool down. It had been a good workout today.

I was pleased with myself. I had made good progress this morning with chapters four and five of my book. Neither was finished, but they were coming along nicely. I liked working on several chapters at the same time. If I hit a blockage at one, I could continue with another until the problem was solved. It was an efficient way of working. My spirits had been excellent after last night. It had been so nice to talk to Steffan... I kept thinking about him. How intelligent he was, how nice a person, and good-looking, too. I would try my best to help him with his investigations. Maybe I had left a positive impression, too? Although I had anticipated his call at lunchtime, the phone had remained silent. Naturally he had been busy, we'd talk later. If he didn't call me, I would take the initiative, maybe tonight, or tomorrow night.

Finished with my cool down, I checked how far Janine had gotten. She was also on a treadmill now, but one further to our right, as the one next to mine had been occupied. She was running full speed. I walked over to tell her I was finished.

"Sue, wait a moment, there is something I need to tell you," she said as I approached, not even out of breath. I waited while she dismounted the still-moving walkway with a gracious jump.

"I meant to tell you this for some time but somehow couldn't find the right moment. The thing is..." she hesitated. "The thing is, I have cancelled my membership. I'm going to move to another part of town and will have to find a new gym for my training. I'm sorry!"

This was news indeed. "So when are you moving?"

"I'm in the middle of it! This is my last training. My apartment must be cleared by the end of this month. So the rest of this week I'll be weightlifting with boxes." She smiled apologetically.

"Well, I wish you luck. And we should keep in touch. May I have your telephone number, or your new address? Would be nice if we met some time again soon. After all, we've shared quite a few drops of sweat, haven't we?" She promised to give me her telephone number in the changing room, while I realized that the initiative to meet again would probably not come from me. I found it hard enough to keep real friendships going, and Janine was only an acquaintance.

We took our towels and went downstairs to shower.

This was a nice gym, the staff was friendly and the place had a female touch. Though both sexes trained here, there was a dressing code for men only: no bare shoulders and no tight shorts. (No such code for women, though, and some girls really displayed their bodies in an inappropriate manner, which I considered slightly unfair.) There were plenty machines for stepping, walking, all-body-training and abdomen exercise, and relatively few for shoulders and weight lifting. As a consequence, there were more women than men attending this gym, and those musclemen who could be so intimidating were mostly absent. With Janine gone, I would have to find another pal to train with.

And this gym was well cleaned, which for me was very important. The only thing that bothered me were the hair clots that sometimes clogged up the drain in the shower. Why was that so revolting to see, I wondered? It was only hair, mixed with soap. Hair was ninety percent keratin, plus a bit of water, fat, minerals and even a trace of vitamins. Nothing to feel disgusted about. While the water poured down my shoulders, I watched the small hair tangle that had collected in a corner of the shower from previous users. Would it be the same in the gent's? Was this a potential source of *Fremdhaar*, foreign hair that a criminal could collect and leave on purpose at a crime scene? Hair from a gym, a swimming pool, a public sauna, it wouldn't be too difficult to collect shed hair and select a few for a crook plan. While I was getting dressed I thought about this, then wished Steffan would ring, so that I could tell him my little theory.

I parted from Janine, wishing her luck with the move and everything.

"Stay the way you are!" were my words after we had hugged. Her long chestnut hair bounced as she walked away with long and graceful strides.

# IX

That night, Robert came home in a bad mood; something to do with his work, problems with finances and wrong politics in his department. I didn't pay much attention to his complaints. He could utter his frustration to the wall if he wanted. He hadn't asked about my progress with my book for days; in fact, he didn't show much evidence that he noticed my presence, or was interested in me, at all. He was completely focussed on his work. Out of the blue, he asked, in quite an accusatory tone, why the lock of the front door had still not been repaired. He added that it was a simple thing to order a locksmith, and couldn't I have… That blew it. I exploded.

"I don't care about that bloody lock. If it is such a simple thing to order a locksmith, why didn't you do it yourself!" I shouted.

"Look, you know I am terribly busy. And may I point out that, in contrast to you, I'm not here during the day. It is much easier for you to grab the telephone and..."

"Busy, is that what you call it? No, you're not here during the day, nor at night, for that matter! Busy, right? Do you think I am an idiot or what? Those long nights in town... You don't think I believe that's related to work, do you?" I became angrier with every word.

"Sue, now, be reasonable. It is not what you think."

"Don't you lie to me!" I was now yelling. It grew into a full-blown row. At one stage I spat out:

"You can do as you please, I no longer care!" and stamped out of the living room, slamming the door behind me.

"Sue, listen, it is not what it seems. It's for your…" but I didn't want to hear. I screamed through the closed door:

"Shut up, you bastard! Leave me alone!" and ran to my room. Why did this guy never know when to shut up?

***

Next morning, I pretended to be asleep when Robert rose to go to his weekly running practice. I only got up after I had heard him leave the house. I was still angry after the fight. He had not apologized, which I thought he should, as it was his fault we had this row. However, if I were completely honest about this, it had not been entirely on his accord only: I had been in a bad mood myself because Steffan had not rung, and I realized that I had felt guilty about being upset for not receiving that call. Which got a train of thoughts going: if Robert hadn't betrayed me, I would never have allowed myself to get emotionally involved with another man. That had set off my explosion. Still, I considered it had mostly been Robert's fault. The more I thought about this, the more nervous I became. My stomach felt as if someone had tied a rope around it. Thinking about Steffan, and the fact that he had not contacted me, made the suffering worse.

Our last evening together had ended with a suspense that I was certain he must have noticed. Although nothing had happened, our parting had been slightly awkward. Was it for that reason that he hadn't kept his promise to ring next day at lunchtime? When eventually the phone rang my pulse started racing. It was him! Although it was Saturday, he called me! My voice trembled when I greeted him, but he sounded neutral, with that sympathetic voice, and stated matter-of-factly:

"Hallo Sue, I wanted to share that bit of information with you that I couldn't remember exactly the other day, about the location of those hairs on the victims. For the first case: one hair was found on her right thigh, inner side. One on the belly, close to the navel. The third was on her left breast. For the second case, one hair was located on the left knee of the woman and the other on her forehead, close to her own hair." I concentrated on what he said, and for a moment forgot about my emotions. Grabbing a piece of paper, I quickly scribbled down these facts, shaking my head in disbelief when I saw my own writing. These were such unusual locations, it could only mean the hairs had been placed there on purpose. My voice sounded normal when I commented:

"Those are very strange locations, indeed! I'm inclined to believe these two cases are the work of one person. The hairs seem to have been placed on the body on purpose. Maybe the murderer is sending us a message, though I wouldn't know what it would mean. I have to think about this."

As an afterthought I asked:

"How much time separated the two murders?"

"That was, let me see, nearly two months. The first case was on December fourth, the second one February first."

I wrote down the dates on the same piece of paper. The facts he had given me were so bizarre that I considered my theory of the origin of stray hairs a futility not worth mentioning anymore.

"I'll call you back when I have any ideas," I said, and hung up. My hand was slightly trembling.

***

I had to finish a table for my chapter five before doing anything else. This table was the major component for that chapter, and once that was finished I could wrap up chapters one to five. I wanted to send these to the publisher soon, as that would pacify them and buy me time. Right now I was fighting with the margins of the table. Some cells contained a lot of text, while others only contained a few words. If I broadened one row so that the filled cells looked fine, it looked wrong for the cells further down that were nearly empty. Besides, other rows became too narrow and too much of their text moved to the next line, elongating the whole table to flow over onto the next page. *Sue, you're wasting your time!* I knew it didn't matter, as the table would eventually be typeset before it was printed, but I wanted the table to look neatly even in my draft. I can be painstakingly perfectionistic with these things.

While I was playing with the layout of my table, I thought of the data written down on the piece of paper next to my telephone, which I now knew by heart:

Case I. 3 black hairs, right thigh, belly, left breast. 4.12
Case II. 2 blond hairs, left knee, forehead. 1.02

I realized this was not all the information I had learned about the two cases. I actually knew more about both crime scenes. Why not put everything together in a table? Being fed up with my fight for the large table of chapter five, I opened a new Word file, drew a table and entered all the data that I knew of, omitting the names of the girls, in the style of Braun:

| Case | Date | Hair colour | Location | | | On body | Strangl. |
|---|---|---|---|---|---|---|---|
| I | 04.12 | black | right thigh | belly | left breast | latex | bra |
| II | 01.02 | blond | left knee | forehead | ? | ? | hands |

*Bitteschön*!

Now I could see what I should ask Steffan next time. Was it possible that in Case II a third hair had been overseen? And had there been latex traces on the victim's body?

Feeling better, I returned to the table of chapter five and promised myself not to spend more than ten minutes on it, no matter how good or bad the result would be. Then I read through the texts I had written last, corrected a few typos and checked if all literature references were correctly cited. I saved the chapter and made backups onto an external drive of all five. Satisfied, I wrote an email to my publisher, included the five chapters as attachment, and pressed 'send'. It felt good: the first five chapters of my book were done! That is to say, their first drafts were handed in, but still, this was a milestone. It was enough for today. *Relax!*

It was time to get out into the fresh air. Time for a biking tour. I checked my bike, pumped up the tyres and oiled the chain. Then I changed into my biking gear and dashed off, forcing all thoughts out of my mind.

***

The message on the answering machine was from Peter Eichholz, my friend the lawyer. He asked if I could call him back, as he needed my advice. Surprised by this unusual request from him, I dialled the number of his *Kanzlei*, and made an appointment through his secretary for tomorrow. I had spent most of this morning in the library of the University. After all, not all literature is available on the web. Instead of making photocopies of the relevant sections from various books (I was using so many of them that the library would not lend them out all at once), I had taken photos using my phone. After transferring the photos to my computer, the texts were perfectly readable on screen, though a bit deformed at the edges, and if needed I could even print them. I spent the rest of this day reading and incorporating this novel knowledge into the next lot of chapters I was working on. Once in a while I picked my mind what Peter would want from me, or when it would be appropriate to call Steffan again. I didn't want to give him the impression I stalked him!

When I showed up in Peter's office next day, he wasn't yet in. His secretary, who remembered me from previous visits although the last one had been more than a year ago, addressed me in English:

"Something urgent at the bar." It took me a moment to realize she didn't mean a bar for drinks, but the court.

He arrived twenty minutes late, in haste and irritated.

"I'm terribly sorry, Sue, didn't want to keep you waiting that long!" he apologized.

I said it wasn't a problem; I had admired the old building where his law firm was seated, with high, decorated ceilings and oil paintings on the walls.

It took him a while, but eventually we were seated in his office and he had organized himself. More courtesies were exchanged, coffee had been ordered and brought in, until finally he made his point.

"I need your advice for a client of mine. The case is delicate." I remembered I had used that phrase not long ago.

"You know you can count on my confidentiality. Do I have to sign anything?" I half joked, though in my business I had frequently signed confidentiality agreements, when I consulted for commercial R&D departments and patents were at stake. Peter smiled at the thought.

"I would rather pretend our conversation never took place," he replied. I understood.

"A client of mine has been accused of using the paid service of women. In fact, of one particular woman with the oldest profession in the world. She was recently found dead..." He paused to see if I understood. I dryly asked:

"Do you mean Lena, the first prostitute, or Laila, the second one murdered in our town?"

"The first. So I guess you can tell who my client is."

I knew he was not supposed to disclose that information. I nodded to indicate I knew we were talking about Reiner Bamberg, the politician who had been in the middle of a steep career until his name was mentioned in connection to the murdered call girl. He had already been mentioned as a candidate minister for the next government, would his party win the elections. The scandal about the link between him and a murdered prostitute did a lot of damage to his and his party's reputation.

"His career has been steep, so far, but now he is in trouble, isn't he?"

Peter elaborately told the story. I don't know many lawyers, but if they were all as wordy as he, one shouldn't wonder that lawsuits might take months to complete. Apparently, Herr Bamberg denied he had ever had anything to do with the killed woman, or with any other prostitute, for that matter. He wanted to prove his innocence quickly, to clear his reputation and limit the damage. He had hired Peter to advise him, and Bamberg came up with the suggestion to do a voluntary DNA test, which would prove him innocent. Peter wanted to know from me whether that was a good idea.

"In general, if he is really innocent, which your client knows best, it would be a smart thing to do. However, in this particular case, it is a bit more complicated." Peter had broken his oath by disclosing information about a client of him. It could cost him his registration if I misused his confidence. I would also have to disclose confidential information to him, and admit I had broken in a laboratory, to explain what the problem was, and I wasn't sure if I wanted him to know this.

To buy a bit of time, I asked for a glass of water. My mind worked quickly. There was a minute chance, negligible but not zero, that this voluntary act of Bamberg could backfire. What if his DNA found a match? By the time Peter came back carrying a bottle of mineral water and two glasses on a tray, I knew what I needed to ask him before giving him my advise.

"The thing I need to know is, has Herr Bam... Has your client ever provided a sample for DNA screening in the past?"

It turned out he had. About five years ago, a young girl had been raped and killed in the neighbourhood where the politician then lived. The police was convinced the murderer had known the girl, but none of her relatives or acquaintances could be identified as a suspect. So there had been a voluntary call to produce a saliva sample, for all men between the age of sixteen and seventy, who lived in her neighbourhood. Reiner Bamberg, who had then been a local councillor, set an example and had his mouth swapped in front of the camera. The action had indeed identified the murderer, which had really surprised me: the culprit had been naive enough to hand in his saliva voluntarily.

"Ah, yes, I remember that case now. Didn't know about the show-off of your client, though. As you know, those saliva samples, their DNA and the resulting DNA fingerprints have long since been destroyed. That was the condition upon which the voluntary action had been granted." I paused for a second. "However..."

What if the fingerprints had not been destroyed? What if Kazinski had not completely rejected Monica's results? What if one of those three hairs had produced a match in the database? A match to the DNA of a well-known politician... Suddenly, I could see a motive why Kazinski had acted the way he had. If he had found this particular match, he could use it to blackmail poor Reiner Bamberg!

"Sue, are you still there?" asked Peter. I had been completely absorbed by my own thoughts. It was extremely unlikely: these were a lot of ifs in this story. But it was not entirely impossible.

"Peter, there is something rotten about the DNA evidence related to that prostitute murder case that your client got involved in. I can't go into the details, I'm sorry, but you'd rather not want to know what I know. Take my word for it: at the moment I would advise against your client giving his DNA voluntarily. There is a minute chance that his DNA could produce a match, even though he could be completely innocent. I know, DNA doesn't lie, but as I said, there is something rotten going on here. I happen to work on this case, off the record, and I will keep your client in mind during my investigations." While I made the promise, I wondered how on earth I was going to find out whether my crazy hypothesis was correct.

"I'll let you know when I learn something that is of relevance to your client. For the moment, I suggest you advice him against handing in a DNA sample," I repeated. Peter looked puzzled, but he didn't ask further questions.

"I hope I'll understand all this once I've read your book!" he joked. I wasn't so certain about that. I couldn't possibly include this example in a scientific book. Even if my scenario were true, nobody would believe the odds!

# X

I was preparing chapter eight, on visualization of forensic information. There is a lot of truth in the saying that a picture says a thousand words, and illustrations can be very helpful to point out the main findings of an investigation or to summarize complex information. However, figures can also be confusing, or even misleading, by accident or intentionally. For example, let's imagine two graphs that each show a curve (of, say, the amount of DNA present in a sample with increasing size), with the left curve reaching much higher levels than the right one. Such a picture is immediately processed by the brain of the observer to mean that the left one is showing something of a bigger value. But few readers will check whether the scale on the axes of both graphs is the same, and if it is not, the curves may be misleading. Well, that sort of stuff. I was writing my way through examples of bad illustrations, pointing out how the reader could identify misleading figures, until I got tired.

My mind drifted back to Steffan and the events of the past few weeks; to Monica's misfortune and our nightly adventure, to Kazinski's fraud and his possible motive, to Peter's client and his DNA that might still be kept in a database somewhere, and to the murder of poor Lena and Laila. What had I just written? Visualization is an important part of communication. I wondered if it helped if I drew a picture of the facts we had collected so far. Why not give it a try? The piece of paper with the location of those hairs was still on my desk.

Using a simple drawing programme I produced two female stick figures and put a cross at the locations where the hairs had been found.

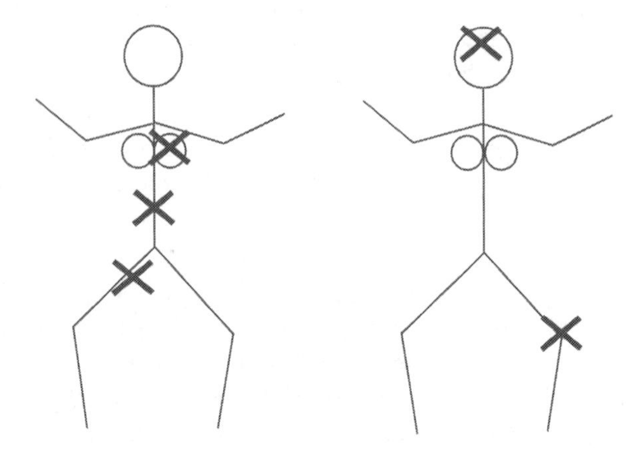

What was this picture showing? For instance, that there was a certain symmetry in the locations of the hairs. The belly button was the central position on the first victim, and the hair on her left breast complemented that on her right thigh. For the second victim, the forehead was the central location. In case there had been a third hair on the body of Laila that had been missed by the crime scene investigators, it could have been placed on her right arm, possibly at the elbow, or the right knee. Either way would restore the symmetry. I would ask Steffan to double-check the photographs of the victim.

There was something else I noticed from my drawing. In the second case, the two hairs were located farther apart than the three hairs of Case I. I encircled the three crosses in my first drawing, and the two in my second. Now it appeared as if the hairs represented a circle that was expanded in the second case. I had the vision of a stone being thrown into a pond, drawing circles on the water surface that grew wider and wider. The murderer wanted to draw ever bigger circles, drawing them with hairs. Hair. Symmetry. Expanding circles. What did it mean? The first case had resulted in the defamation of a politician, so it drew a circle bigger than 'just' a murder. Would the customers of Laila be even more influential, and would that case draw even bigger circles? *You're imagining things, Sue, don't try to be a profiler, that is a specialist's job.* With a sigh, I turned my concentration on my chapter eight again.

***

That weekend was *Fasching*, and carnival is a big event in this part of Germany. It had already started on the Thursday of the week before the start of Lent with *'Weiberfasching'*, a special day on which most parties are organized for women only. Every city has its own traditions, but in the area where we live, men should rather not wear a tie on that Thursday, as many women, armed with scissors, are waiting for the opportunity to cut off that symbol of power. At the university, a professor would wear his oldest tie (or his latest Christmas present, in case it wasn't his taste) until some female student would cut off the lower half. For the rest of the day, the professor would proudly walk with the truncated tie around his neck as a sign of obedience. From Saturday till Tuesday of *Fasching*, a trip by train could be a torture, unless sharing a wagon with a group of drunken adolescents, brawling and yelling (or worse) is something to your liking. Schools and many shops would be closed for two or three days and even at the university teaching was halted. Since this meant that Robert didn't have to go into work, and both of our sons had a few days off, the whole family gathered at home.

It was nice to have the house full of men again. The boys had not visited us since the Christmas holidays, and brought home stories of parties, heartbreak (of their friends, of course, they would never share their own mishap on the path of love with their parents) and rock concerts. I didn't dare to ask if they had any time left to spend on their studies. At least, with all this bustle, I didn't have to think about my book for a few days, which, together with murders, DNA evidence, and matrimonial fights was buried away to the back of my head. It was a welcome break to the past two months.

Every city had its own day for the big carnival parade, so depending on where you went, you could visit one on Saturday, Monday or Tuesday. In our city, the *Faschingsumzug* is traditionally held on Monday, and this year I decided to go and watch it. *Fasching* was very late this year, with reasonable weather as a consequence: mild temperatures and a weak sun, instead of sleet and snow like we had last year. The carnival float was accompanied by musical bands and the majority of spectators were disguised, to various degrees. Some of the onlookers wore elaborate costumes with accompanying makeup, while for others a brightly coloured scarf or a funny hat would do. Alcohol was present everywhere, and many people were tipsy, even though it wasn't even past midday. Children collected sweets that were liberally strewn from the float wagons. The displays on the float trucks were inspired by local politics. One depicted poor Reiner Bamberg, with an enormous erection (hidden by an oversized pair of trousers) chasing a woman in sexy lingerie.

The news on the night of Carnival Tuesday brought me back to my investigations. It turned out I got confirmation of my hypothesis of the increasing impact of hairs left on murder victims sooner than I had dreamed of. That night, the national television news presented an item about a Captain of Industry who was somehow involved in the case of a murdered prostitute. The drawing I had produced a few days ago swam before my eyes. Expanding circles. There was a serial killer at play, and I had entered his playground. Whether he wanted or not, I was part of his game.

***

Steffan shook his head. He had systematically checked the photographs with a magnifying glass, but he had not been able to find a third hair on the body of dead Laila. He offered me to have a look, but I quickly refused. I was not used to looking at photographs of killed bodies. I had never liked working with human body parts in a lab, at least not if the material could still be clearly identified as such, and a photo of a victim was just as bad. I could never have been a pathologist. We were seated in his office, with the door closed. After I had called him last night and informed him of my hypothesis, he no longer cared about my official status, or lack thereof. My suggestion that the killer had maybe collected hairs from some public shower was welcomed with approval. When I asked if traces of latex had been found on the second victim, he replied that I was spot on: the positive results from the lab had come in that morning. But I had to accept that the other question mark in my table drew a negative: a third hair had not been found.

"Maybe the killer was disturbed, and couldn't finish his job?" I proposed.

"We don't know. Let's accept the fact that two hairs were found. We can expect the DNA fingerprints of the blond hairs to be different to those of the black hairs, right?"

"Yes, I think so. Unless these hairs have not always been blond. They may have been treated with $H_2O_2$ – *in situ* or *in vitro.*"

“*Entschuldigung*?” Without realizing, I had turned to lab jargon that he was not familiar with.

“I mean, it could be that the hairs had been bleached with hydrogen peroxide, either on the head, or after separation from the scalp. Hydrogen peroxide is the active ingredient that is used to bleach hair. Even black hair can be turned blond if you bleach it long enough. But then one can no longer detect any DNA, as it would have been destroyed by the radicals that peroxide produces.” I hoped that was clearer – how much chemistry would a chief inspector remember from his days in school?

“I think the location of those hairs may provide further clues. Look at this,” I showed him the picture I had drawn, and talked him through my theory of expanding circles. He studied my crude drawing with interest.

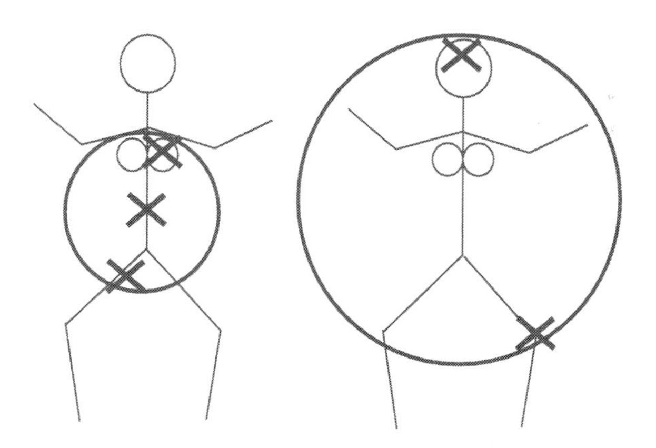

Eventually he commented: “You may be right, the location of the hairs may be the clue, not so much their fingerprint. You know what, I no longer care whether the identical DNA fingerprints that Kazinski had put in his report were accurate or not. I can’t be bothered by those fake results, but I do appreciate that you discovered his fraud, because now we are making progress. Tomorrow morning I will present this theory about the significance of the location of these hairs at our team meeting. Expanding circles. I like that allegory. It fits with the events of last night. The media are making a real fuzz about it.”

I didn’t like the idea that Kazinski would get away with his fraud that easily, but I didn’t want to oppose Steffan. His last remark reminded me of the other question I had for him:

"Do you know how they found out? I mean, how did the press know about that politician, Bamberg, related to the first case, and now this businessman… I wonder where they got that information from?"

"You can't imagine what a scene we've had this morning," he replied. "Our team members have been accused of leaking to the press. Unheard of! And as far as I know, this whole accusation is completely speculative. There is no evidence that I know of that this business guy had been affiliated to the woman."

Interesting. The press released a connection that even the chief inspector was not aware of, and despite this, his team members were being accused of leaking to the press.

"Do you have the name of the journalist who presented the scoop?"

"Which one do you mean, the one who wrote about Bamberg, or the second one, that hit the news last night?"

I would like to follow up on both. A journalist would never reveal his source to the police, and certainly not if that source were a leak from within the investigation team. But maybe he (or she) would talk to me, especially if I offered something in return. It was worth a try. And maybe I could even indirectly assist in the defence of Peter's poor client.

# XI

The names of the journalists were written in a small, slanted handwriting, with tall upper strokes that were applied with heavy pressure on the pen. A graphologist would conclude the writer was self-confident, in control, dominant, ambitious. *No, stop analysing his handwriting, concentrate on what you're doing!* His words had repeated in my head: *I can't be bothered by those fake results.* Kazinski's fraud was of no importance to Steffan. All that mattered to him was that he solved his cases, and that the evidence would be accepted in court. But I had my own priorities. If Kazinski would get away with this, who could guarantee that he wouldn't fabricate data in future cases? The reputation of forensic investigations was at stake here!

I looked at the names of the journalists again. One of them I recognized: it was the guy who had asked me for a radio interview on 'CSI-like investigations'. What would be the best way to approach him? A bad idea had presented itself. It was wicked, dangerous even. It wasn't my way to play with facts like this. My own reputation could suffer. But it might be the only way to find out how that journalist had discovered the link between the murdered prostitute and Reiner Bamberg.

I checked his homepage from the website of the news programme he worked for to find his contact data, and dialled his number to make an appointment.

***

Matthias Dornfeld had agreed to meet in the lobby of a hotel in town. When I arrived he wasn't there yet, so I waited with a coffee on the table in front of me, observing guests who were checking out, and watching a cleaner leisurely polishing the marble floor of the reception hall.

Finally the journalist entered the lobby. He looked as if he had spent too many late hours in a bar. His face was pale and narrow, and bags showed under his eyes. His thin hair was untidy, and a small moustache gave him a Slavic look. He wore dirty jeans and a leather jacket that showed grease stains on the collar and at the cuffs. He recognized me from the description I had given of myself, and after shaking hands he sat down, still panting from his hasty entry.

I had told him on the telephone that I had information related to the case of the killed prostitute. He had not asked further questions then. Now he looked inquisitive and waited till I began.

"For a start, I want to stress that the source of this information must not be released," I began, though I knew this was the unwritten rule of journalism anyway.

"Do you mind if I take notes?" he asked, taking a Moleskin notebook out of his inner pocket.

"Second, I want something in return for my information," I continued, ignoring his interruption. I didn't care if he took notes, but he needed to understand my conditions. And I realized it would eventually become obvious who the source was of what he was going to learn. Only five people knew about this, and once this went public, the insiders would quickly deduce who had talked to the press.

"Well, you'll have to be a bit more specific before I can promise you anything," he replied cautiously. At least he didn't terminate our conversation immediately. I presented the next fragment of my story, which I needed to dose carefully:

"I can provide you a scoop, in return for which I want to know how you got information about the victim's clientele."

He inhaled sharply and his eyes narrowed.

'"You know that I have to protect my sources. You've just asked for that yourself!" I knew he would say this, and I had anticipated how to react.

"How much is a story worth about manipulation of forensic evidence, and potential blackmail of a public figure?" Maybe that would warm him up. His eyes narrowed.

"And what will you do with the information of my source, if I were to give it to you in return?" he reposted. I could feel the heat already.

"I will not make it public and not share it with the police."

"So why do you want to know?"

"I said my story is potentially about blackmail. If my theory is correct, there may be a connection between this blackmail and your source, the person that let you feature Bamberg's relation to the victim. If I'm right, you could deepen that story with a follow-up. It would destroy the reputation of the blackmailer, which is my motive. This isn't about love and peace, you know."

I could see he was considering my offer.

He put away his notebook and crossed his arms.

"OK, out with it. I will confirm when there is a connection between your story and my source after I've heard it. If, however, you're wrong and there is no connection, your story is worthless and I don't have to give you anything in return. Deal?"

I could live with that.

Dornfeld listened attentively as I told him about the manipulation of DNA fingerprints that were obtained from the crime scene. I didn't give him all the details: he didn't have to know about the three hairs, or about their location on the victim's body. What I did tell him was that stains from the *Tatort* had been analysed in Kazinski's Forensic Institute, but the results that he subsequently reported to the police had been manipulated. Naturally, Dornfeld wanted to know how I knew. I explained I had been present when the experiments had been repeated, in an excursion that literally could not see the light of day. He didn't even blink at that.

"I know that two DNA fingerprints obtained from the crime scene have been withheld from the police. My theory is that one of these produced a hit in the DNA database, and that this hit is the origin of the rumour that Bamberg had dealings with this prostitute. You may know that Bamberg had once voluntarily given a saliva sample to the police. His DNA fingerprint should have been destroyed, but it is possible it wasn't. If my theory is correct, I believe that Dr. Kazinski is blackmailing Bamberg."

The journalist took out his notebook again and started writing. My story was complicated, and he needed to put the key points on paper before he could grasp it. I knew that feeling: I could also think clearer with a piece of paper in front of me. I waited patiently.

"If I'm following you, you're speculating that this Kazinski was the source of my information, right?" I nodded, hoping for an affirmation of my theory. He eyed me with a shrewd look.

"Well, I'm sorry to disappoint you, but I think you're wrong," he finally said.

"Why do you say 'you think'? You know your source, don't

you?"

"Not exactly. I received an anonymous letter that stated Bamberg had seen the prostitute, and had visited her the night she was killed. When I investigated I couldn't find definite evidence, but Bamberg had not been home that night, so the story was plausible. These things are difficult to prove; the chick didn't quite publish records of her clients, you know. But it was plausible, and when I presented the story it was only speculative. Of course, colleagues ran away with it, and so the story grew. That's how it works in my profession."

What a lousy excuse. His whole story had been based on an anonymous letter. A letter that could have come from Kazinski, or from anybody else who wanted to ruin Bamberg's reputation. I started to feel nervous. This wasn't developing the way I had hoped.

"I like your story, though," Dornfeld commented with an unpleasant undertone. I bet he did. But I had handed it to him without getting anything in return that made me any wiser. Publication of this blackmail theory would not only damage Kazinski's reputation, but also mine. Of those who knew about his fraud, Gudrun and Monica would never talk; Steffan could easily guess I had leaked to the press, and he wouldn't be pleased about it.

"Unfortunately, what you gave me in return is pretty useless!" I replied, irritated. "You can't rule out blackmail, but anybody could have written that anonymous letter. I assume you won't show it to me?" He just laughed. I had to repair the damage I had done quickly.

"Look, I have given you enough material for a short article, and that can indeed hurt Kazinski. But I didn't get anything back for it, and you knew from the beginning of our conversation that you couldn't tell me your source." He showed a cold smile. I continued:

"All I'm asking now is that you wait a few days with this publication. After all, this first murder has now gone stale. The latest developments with the second murder are far more interesting. What if I investigate a little bit further into that, and I keep you informed? In contrast to what the police has stated, I think that the two murders are indeed connected. Wouldn't that make a much nicer story?"

He stared at his notes again. He was calculating. How much was this story worth as he had written it down, and what were the risks if he kept it under his hat for a few days while the whole thing developed into something with more impact?

"OK, I will wait one week at the most. Let's see if you can find out anything about the second case. Would be nice, if you could give me a clue for a connection. But no games behind my back, you understand?"

He didn't have to worry that I would release the same information to another journalist. I had burned my fingers this once, that wouldn't happen again!

***

On my way back home I tried to decide whether this had gone completely bad, or whether I had actually gotten something positive out of it. I was disappointed that my theory could not be proven, though it had also not been dismissed. Kazinski could still be blackmailing Bamberg. But was he the author of that anonymous letter? Come to think of it, would that be a logical act, if he were indeed blackmailing his victim? By releasing to the press what he knew, he would more or less invalidate his own case. Once the story was out in the open, Bamberg could no longer be blackmailed for having contact with a prostitute. But the DNA evidence had not been published, at least not yet. Was that the pressure Kazinski was using on his victim, and was publication of the connection between Bamberg and Lena his way to tighten the screws? Or was my theory all wrong, and had Kazinski had nothing to do with that letter Dornfeld had received?

I needed to know if there was another anonymous letter, this time sent to another journalist, stating that an influential CEO had had contact with a girl called Laila who was now dead. The question was, how was I going to find out?

# XII

It turned out to be more difficult to get in touch with the second journalist than with Herr Dornfeld. When I called his newsagent, I wasn't put through; instead, a secretary informed me that Herr Thomas Schramm was out, and I could leave a message if I wanted. I requested if he could call me back as soon as possible, and said I would try again this afternoon if I didn't hear from him before then.

In the meantime I collected more information on the defamed businessman. His name was Florian Helmuth, and his present position was Chief Executive Officer of a company producing machine parts. The German export is heavily dependent on companies like his, and Germany is second after leading country Japan for exporting machine tools worldwide. Under Helmuth's reign two smaller firms had recently been swallowed, which increased the size and value of his enterprise considerably; his was now one of the leading brand names in the DAX stock exchange.

It always surprised me how easily these CEOs could change jobs. Helmuth had led, before his life in machine parts, a company specialized in office software, and he had made a success out of that, too. Apparently, it didn't matter what the firm he was managing sold or produced; it was his job, and he was very good at that, to make the trade profitable and let the company grow.

The tanned face of Florian Helmuth (which sharply contrasted with his fair hair) had often been on television; he smiled his bleached smile into the camera whenever there was news about a planned merge or novel profit figures were announced. Because he was so well known, the news that he had had ties to a prostitute, a killed prostitute even, was of national importance. The release of this gossip had caused a considerable dip in the stocks of his company, so that it was even of economic importance that he had presumably paid for sex with a person whose fate it became to be murdered.

The press releases didn't give data on when or how often he had visited the woman. Most of the items presented on television were speculative, with lots of *'hätte'* and *'wäre'*, these useful 'could' and 'might' verbs that sound so beautiful in German subjunctive, and that protect any journalist from being accused of presenting misleading information. After all, nothing was stated as facts, rather, things *could* be true, something *might* have happened, it *may* be possible that…

I reviewed the news items of the past few days in order to find out how much sound evidence there was that Florian Helmuth had indeed had contact with the prostitute, but none of the broadcasts provided more than hints and insinuations.

Finally I got hold of the journalist who had started this all, Thomas Schramm. Not because he called me back, but because, after calling her time after time, his secretary probably was fed up and put me through. Herr Schramm refused to meet me: he was too busy. When I insisted he said he had five minutes for me.

I didn't like to discuss my case over the telephone. Without a means to read his facial expression or his body language, it was hard to find the right words. But this was the only chance I got.

"Herr Schramm, the reason I contacted you is that I have a question related to your story about Herr Florian Helmuth. I realize you don't know me, which makes this seem as a strange request. However, you can check my credentials on the Internet. I am a scientist and I'm specialized in forensic evidence, which got me interested in the two recent murder cases in our city. During my investigations, which I carry out for my own interest, I stumbled upon something which I think could be of potential importance to solve these cases, but I need confirmation. I accept that you need to protect your sources."

I gave him a second to digest this information. It was so much harder over the telephone! Since he didn't say anything, I continued: "I would like to ask you a question that you only have to answer with 'yes' or 'no'. I will keep that information confidential, you don't have to be afraid it will be published or forwarded to a third party. It is for the sake of truth that I ask your collaboration. Can you accept that?"

"It depends on the nature of your question…" was his careful reply.

"I understand. So here it is. Was the information about Helmuth being related to the recent murder brought to you in the form of an anonymous letter?" There was silence on the other end of the line. I gave him time. He was probably thinking about the consequences of providing me an answer, whether affirmative or negative.

"May I ask you how you got to this question?"

"That is problematic. You have to protect your sources, but I have also promised confidentiality to certain individuals. I can't tell you more, I'm sorry. However, if your answer to my question is negative, in other words, if your source was not an anonymous letter, then we can both forget this conversation. In that case I apologize for taking up your time." Again he didn't say anything, but he didn't end the call. That already gave him away. I concluded he had probably received an anonymous letter to disclose the alleged connection between Laila and the Captain of Industry Florian Helmuth.

"I still want to know what you will do with the knowledge, once I answer your question!" he insisted.

"If your answer were 'yes', it would mean yours is the second anonymous letter received in relation to a recent crime. That would give me a clue in understanding particular criminal activities, but I insist that I won't mention your statement to the police, or to anybody else!" I hoped this convinced him. He thought for another moment, then responded, in a soft voice:

"My answer to your question is affirmative. It was an anonymous letter that got me on the lead." He cleared his throat and continued, a bit louder now: "But I have your word that you won't disclose this to anybody. In return, I'd like to know if the other letter you seem to know of had led to the disclosure of Reiner Bamberg being involved in the first murder?" This journalist was not stupid.

"That is a good guess, but in return for my sealed lips, it would only be fair if you kept this knowledge to yourself as well." I just hoped he was not only intelligent, but also honest. I added:

"At least, please keep this silent for one week. Can we agree on that?" He said we could. I hoped he wasn't lying. We ended our telephone conversation after I had left my number, for the umpteenth time, but now directly to him instead of his secretary.

Now I had a moratorium of one week, from two journalists. It gave me some time, but not a lot, to solve these cases without breaking my promise. In order to play fair, I did call Matthias Dornfeld once again to inform him there had been a second anonymous letter. Of course he wanted to know more, but I said I hadn't disclosed anything about the letter he had received, and wouldn't disclose more about the other letter to him. I could tell he worked it out for himself. Both journalists, Dornfeld and Schramm, realized the source of each other's scoop had been an anonymous letter. Once more I insisted on the week's silence from his part, and just hoped for the best.

***

That evening I found my Mac had frozen in the middle of chapter eight, the chapter on visualization of data. Some programme had caused interference, or Word had not been able to cope with the multitude of figures embedded in that text. I couldn't remember if I had saved my latest edits – I hoped I had. Using a shortcut, I killed the programme and decided to reboot the system. Slowly, one window after another closed (I always have lots of windows open at the same time, and too many programs. No wonder the poor system got confused at some point!), until finally the hard disk stopped humming and the computer died. I restarted the whole thing, checked my email inbox (there were no new messages since the last one I had opened: an email from Thomas Schramm that had only said 'I have checked your website, check mine here' but when I had clicked on the link he had provided I got an error404), and then reopened Word to see if any of my latest files had been damaged. Only one file had not been saved – a rescued version opened automatically. It was the table I had made to summarize the evidence of the two murder cases. Realizing the table was now outdated, I modified it with the extra information that I had learned since, and for the sake of being systematic, I saved it properly. Now it read:

| Case | Date | Nr. of hairs | Hair colour | Location | | | On body | Strangl. |
|---|---|---|---|---|---|---|---|---|
| I | 04.12 | 3 | black | right thigh | belly | left breast | latex | bra |
| II | 01.02 | 2 | blond | left knee | fore-head | - | latex | hands |

I considered adding the information about the blackmail, but decided to restrict the table to facts, not including speculations or hypotheses.

I stared at my screen. A serial killer doesn't stop voluntarily.

Would there be another murder in the near future? I am not superstitious, but I couldn't make myself add another line, for a Case III that had not yet been committed, though possibly was part of a bigger plan. If I extrapolated the data that the table summarized, could I predict some of the circumstances if there was going to be a third murder? Let's see what happened if these killings followed the rules of mathematics: Case III would have only one hair deposited on the body of the victim. The hair colour could be red, or any other colour than black or blond, to continue the variation seen this far. The location of that hair would have to be at the utmost extremity of the body, a foot maybe? That would enforce the expanding circles statement. The killer would again wear latex, to avoid leaving traces of himself at the crime scene. He would use an alternative weapon for strangulation, that could be anything, a rope, a belt, a cord, whatever. But what about the date? In many cases the period between the killings by a serial killer decreased over time, as a psychopath would slowly lose control over his craving for the deed. That would mean we could expect another murder soon. I stared at the numbers.

Case I, on 04.12, with three hairs deposited on the body of the victim.

Case II, on 01.02, with two hairs left at the scene. These cases were separated by fifty-nine days. By extrapolation, a Case III would present itself with one hair only, possibly sooner than sixty days after the first of February. That would be before the end of March. I wrote down, not in the table but on a piece of scrap paper: Case III, on XX.03, 1 hair.

The next murder could possibly take place before the first of April, unless the killer could be stopped. If only I could think the same way this crook thought. *There must be a pattern, Sue, try to recognize the pattern!*

The human mind is extremely well equipped to recognize patterns. We see patterns, recognize connections, and identify relations even where there are none. It is one of the reasons why people tend to be superstitious. 'It can't be a coincidence that this accident happened on Friday thirteenth!' (One never notices anything special for bad luck occurring on Tuesday tenth.) 'I thought about my niece only this morning, and now we met on the market!' (How often do you think of a person without meeting him or her the same day?) We often notice connections that don't exist. Scientists are cautious about this, and use statistics to calculate how likely a correlation of data is caused by an underlying cause: statistical calculations can identify if those data just appear to be correlating by more than chance alone. Scientific data are usually reported with a confidentiality of ninety-five percent, which means that, out of one hundred of such observations, five would be caused by chance. Knowing all this, I still believed there was a pattern in these murder cases; one that I had to identify, but for which statistics were useless.

I diverted my thoughts away from this. I knew my brain would work on this puzzle in the background, like a Unix computer performing calculations that you can switch to the background with one simple '&' command. I had to think of other things, and then, possibly, the solution would present itself.

On my way to the kitchen, heading for the fridge to check what I could make for dinner, I discovered the clue. Twelve divided by four gives three. Two divided by one gives two. Three divided by three gives one. The month of the murder divided by the day gives the number of hairs. If that were the pattern here, the next killing would be on the third of March... But that couldn't be! It was March twelfth today! Had a third murder already taken place and had it so far remained unnoticed? Was the body of a murdered prostitute laying somewhere, decomposing, waiting to be discovered? A slight nausea developed. I grabbed the phone and called Steffan, asking for an urgent meeting. Then I continued with my writing, promising myself to write at least half a chapter before the end of this week. With a sigh, I logged back in to my computer and tried to be productive.

# XIII

The recent events prevented me from making much progress with my writing. I found it hard to concentrate. I missed being able to talk to Robert about my theories and doubts. It always helped to have to phrase one's thoughts into comprehensible sentences; for me it felt as if I ordered my brain while I talked things through with my husband. But Robert wasn't there to act as a sound box. He was staying in Geneva, Switzerland, to discuss some experiments that were planned for the Large Hadron Collider, the particle accelerator built by the European consortium CERN. He had left soon after the carnival weekend and we had only half-heartedly conciliated our fight. I wasn't sure how to react once he came back from his travels. I was still mad at him because of his cheating, and every time I thought of this my anger grew. Jealousy is a feeling that feeds itself, enforcing itself every time it pops up in the mind.

And that was not the only nagging thought I suffered from. My mind kept returning to the actions of Kazinski, to the anonymous letters that I still presumed he had written. My theory made it plausible why he had written the first, but what motive did he have to inform Schramm with the second letter? Or was Kazinski not the sender, and were the letters sent by the killer? Was Kazinski the murderer? No, that was ridiculous. He wouldn't have a motive! I didn't like the guy, but I couldn't imagine him to be a serial killer. But then, how do you recognize a psychopath? Of one thing I was convinced: that both anonymous letters had been sent by one and the same person. Since the first accusation had been false (Reiner Bamberg was innocent, why else would he want to voluntarily hand in a DNA sample?), I presumed the second accusation, that of CEO Florian Helmuth being involved with the second victim, to be untrue as well.

I kept flipping from one theory to the other: either Kazinski was the author of those letters, or the murderer had sent them. I wouldn't accept the third option, that Kazinski and the killer were one and the same person. And I dismissed the possibility outright that the letters had nothing to do with either Kazinski or the murderer.

I reconsidered my assumption that Kazinski was blackmailing Bamberg. That was likely only if he had identified a match in an illegally stored DNA database. After all, the DNA sample that Bamberg had provided to the police five years ago should have been destroyed, together with all electronic files of his DNA fingerprints. I needed to know if such a database existed.

That evening I called Monica, under the pretension to ask how she liked her new job. She sounded cheerful: the work was fine, the colleagues were nice, and she got on well with her new boss.

It was with reluctance that I reminded her of her previous work environment, but it had to be.

"Monica, there is something I need to know about the Forensic Institute. Did you search the DNA database for matches yourself, or was that done by your supervisor?"

"I usually did that myself, if the fingerprints were of sufficient quality."

"And did one of those three hair samples provide a match in the database?" She had never said so, but then, I had never asked.

"No, all three were unique. There was no hit identified in the database beyond the threshold."

It didn't rule out anything. It could be that Kazinski kept a backup of an extended DNA database somewhere, an illegal database in which he kept profiles that should have been deleted. Then I thought of something else.

"One more question, my dear. When exactly did you report your results to Dr. Kazinski? Can you remember the date?"

She considered. It had been a Friday, and it was shortly before Christmas. I quickly did the calculations. Last year's Christmas Eve, *Heiligabend* which in Germany is the start of Christmas, had been a Thursday. Typically, on December 24th all shops close early afternoon, to reopen only on the 27th. This past year, the shops remained closed even till the 28th, as Boxing Day was followed by a Sunday – I remembered how difficult it had been to buy food to cater for all these holidays, while the shops had been overflowed with late Christmas shoppers. So, if Monica had handed in her data on the Friday before Christmas, that must have been December 18th. That could be important! I thanked her elaborately, and wished her all the best in her new job. It could well be that I had just received a clue that, if I followed up on this, could rule out one hypothesis; I had identified a way to disprove that Kazinski was behind those letters, if he had not been the author. I couldn't prove it if he was, but by dismissing one theory after another, one can also get closer to the truth. It was a start and it felt like progress.

***

I had wanted to talk to Matthias Dornfeld before meeting up with Steffan, but this time it was this journalist who was out of reach. He neither answered his telephone nor an urgent email message that I sent him. Since I had urged Steffan for a meeting, he had suggested I come over to his office at the end of the day – now I couldn't postpone. There was still enough we had to discuss. Last time we had exchanged ideas we had concentrated on the location of the found hairs on the bodies of the two victims. It seemed ages ago, though less than a week had passed since then. I reckoned I had made a lot of progress with my investigations, and was excited to tell him about it. (Secretly I hoped he would be impressed). Moreover, I was dying to learn what he and his team had discovered.

We were seated opposite each other, Steffan behind his desk while I had taken the visitor's chair in front of it. It felt formal and distant, as if he deliberately wanted to create some space between us. I decided to ignore the meaning of that setting for the moment; getting the facts on the table was more important.

I told him what I had found out from the two journalists. I realized that, by doing so, I was breaking my promise to them, but Steffan couldn't use my information in his official investigations anyway. We were still exchanging ideas under the condition that our conversations had never taken place. He nodded in approval when I told about the two anonymous letters, though I didn't tell him what I had given the journalists in return, or that they had promised a moratorium of one week only. My theory that both letters were likely to be written by the same person was again received with a nod. However, from his face I could tell he didn't approve the possibility that Kazinski would be blackmailing Reiner Bamberg, though he accepted that the politician's DNA profile could, at least in theory, still reside in some database. Next, I stated the options of who could have sent those letters, counting them off my fingers: *1*, the anonymous letters had been written by the killer, which added weight to what we had called the 'Expanding Circles Theory'; *2*, the letters had been written by Kazinski, for reasons of blackmail, or (I mentioned it although I knew he wouldn't agree) *3*, that Kazinski was the author and the killer. As expected, Steffan shook his head now.

"I don't consider option number three likely, either, but we have to discuss all possibilities," I hastened to say. I had left out possibility number 4, that neither the killer nor Kazinski had anything to do with the letters; apparently, Steffan didn't notice.

But that was not all I had to tell.

I showed him a printout of the table in which I had summarized the facts of the murder Cases I and II. I had still not added a third row to fill in with hypothetical Case III, but I talked him through my extrapolations.

"So, if there is a mathematical logic in these crimes, and if we continue that logic for a hypothetical third case, we can expect that one hair would be left on the victim, possibly of a different colour again, let's say red this time. I don't know what the Expanding Circles Theory would predict, but we should be prepared for the worst, again starting with an anonymous letter to the press. The most crucial extrapolation, in my opinion, is if we can predict the date of a third case. But unfortunately, that is where I get lost."

I explained the formula of day divided by month giving the numbers of hairs left on the body.

"If this is what is going on here, the next murder should have taken place on the third of March, to be marked with one hair only. But there hasn't been a murder in the past two weeks, has there? At least, none was discovered. What do you think, is there a body lying somewhere that we don't know about?"

Steffan rolled his eyes. He explained that prostitutes normally get visitors more often than once every two weeks, and that a body would start to smell by then, even in winter, if it were lying in a heated room. He thought it extremely unlikely that there had been a murder in town that had remained unnoticed. I agreed, though it shot holes in my extrapolation theory. If the date couldn't be predicted, how valid were my other predictions? And even if they were accurate, how could that knowledge help us?

It was the Chief Inspector's turn to reveal what he and his team had found out. As a consequence of the new working hypothesis that the two murders were the result of a serial killer, his team had tried to find a connection between the two women. Neither of them had worked for an organization or a procurer. Both of them had advertised their services in the Internet, but they used different portals. There was no evidence that they had known each other.

"Could they share clients, you think?"

It was possible, but there was no evidence of that, either.

"So do you think it was a complete coincidence that these two prostitutes were selected, and it might just as well have been two different women?" I asked in disbelief. To be in the wrong place at the wrong time, with death by strangulation as a consequence; it gave me the shivers. But I couldn't quite imagine that the victims had not specifically been singled out. That wasn't at all what I would have expected from a killer who seemed to have planned his deeds so carefully.

"We simply don't know. Right now we're checking telephone and credit cards records to see if there is any connection or shared activities between the two victims. They didn't use the same bank, or the same insurance companies… we've already ruled out a lot of possibilities. It is a task that is frustratingly time-consuming."

I realized it was. It was like providing evidence in the lab that something was not possible. How many times did one have to try, how many variables did one have to test, before negative evidence would be convincing? Maybe there was no connection between the women indeed. Steffan said they were still digging in the computers of both victims, in the hope to find a common clue that way. He had also sent out a request for information to all other police stations in our *Bundesland*, in case the killer was active in other cities as well. He seemed to be slightly frustrated by lack of progress, and I couldn't blame him. There was a lot of pressure on him to resolve these murders as soon as possible.

When it was time for me to leave I considered for a moment to invite him for a drink, but it was better to keep our contact professional. He gave me his card again, this time with a webmail address written on it.

"In case you need to get in touch other than by telephone," he explained. "But please, keep it discrete."

I felt slightly sad on my way home, though I wasn't sure whether it was out of pity for Steffan because of his lack of progress, or because we had parted without as much as a hug.

# XIV

Apart from feeling sad, I was also frustrated. The questions of this afternoon kept replaying in my head on my way home, like a tape on auto-rewind. Who had sent the anonymous letters to the press? Why was my prediction of the date for a third murder wrong? Would there be a third case at all? After all, extrapolation from two sets of data is a bit pushing. How did the killer select his victims? Without thinking, I parked my car in front of the house, at its regular parking spot, although Robert was still in Switzerland and he had taken his car, so I could have parked mine in the garage (we only had a single garage, and had never bothered to enlarge it for two cars). Since I had already stopped the engine, I didn't bother. While I was walking up to the house, I noticed something weird: our front door was open! I knew the lock was buggy, but the door shouldn't be open like that! No lights shone inside, thus it wasn't Robert who had unexpectedly come home. I halted in the middle of the path leading up to the door. Could it be that someone was in the house? Was this a burglary? Fear started to creep up from my stubborn feet, producing wobbly knees and a pounding heart beat. What should I do? I remembered the piece of advice I had once received from a security guard when I had asked him what would be the best thing to do if there were a burglar in the house. *Keep his exit free!* A thief easily panics, and when disturbed he wants to leave the place as quickly as possible. Block his exit and you might be in trouble. If I now went through that door, and if someone was still inside, I would be in his way in case he stormed out. Or they, maybe there was a gang roaming through my things! With trembling fingers I pulled my phone out of my pocket to call the police. For an instant I thought of calling Steffan, but he was working at the *Mordkommission*, not exactly the correct department to deal with private burglaries. I hesitated between dialling 110 and 112 – which was the fire alarm and which was the police number again? *Stay calm, Sue!*

"*Guten Abend, Frau* Callighan!" I jumped at the sound of the voice behind me. It was our neighbour down the road, Herr Stein, the locksmith, who was walking his dog. His big body slightly swayed with every step, moving his impressive weight from one leg to another, as he dragged his also overweight dog behind him. I dashed towards him.

"Oh Herr Stein, I'm so pleased to see you! Please can you help me? I just came home and found my front door open. I'm afraid there has been a burglary. I don't dare to go in…" it may have sounded feeble, but in instances like these, a woman needs a man to hide behind. At least, I do. And Stein was a big man to use as a shield!

He walked up the open door without fear, and peeked at the lock.

"I don't see any sign of breaking in," he commented dryly.

'I know, the lock was not working properly. I meant to ask you to have a look at it for ages, but I kept forgetting. However, I'm certain I closed the door behind me. Do you mind if we check together to see if everything is all right?"

Herr Stein didn't reply but let his dog on the loose (who started sniffing around my garden with a sudden interest for these otherwise forbidden grounds) and just walked in, begging me to follow. I kept close to his heels. The kitchen was empty and looked just like I had left it. The living room seemed undisturbed, too. I hesitated leading Herr Stein to our bedroom (I didn't know him that well); instead, I guided him towards the left, to my office. When I stepped in behind him, I saw immediately that someone had been there. The drawers of my desk had been pulled open, and some papers were strewn on the floor. My stomach contracted when I saw the gaping emptiness where my computer should have been.

"My laptop is gone!" I cried, and covered my mouth with my hand in disbelief. Herr Stein put an arm around me.

"Calm there, now. *Alles gut*."

But it was not going to be all right. Nothing was all right! My computer was an essential part of me, I often joked I stored my brain in that machine. My work was in there. When was the last backup I had made? And what else might they have stolen? Bewildered, I looked around me. Herr Stein squeezed me gently and then he let go of my shoulder.

"You shouldn't touch anything right now. Let me quickly check the rest of the house to make sure they aren't still here. *Geht's*?" Yes, I was calmer now. I just stood there, frozen in my office, slightly shaking, trying to think of what else could have been of value to the thieves. Herr Stein was back before I knew it.

"They're gone, don't worry. You have to inform the police. And don't worry about that computer. That is a case for your insurance company." But that was the trouble.

"Insurance? You just said there were no traces of breaking in. This is going to be difficult."

Herr Stein looked at me with a pitiful expression. "I guess it will be, considering that you knew the lock was faulty..." His remark made me feel even more miserable, and guilty too. If only I had called him earlier, and had the lock repaired in time... "If you're sure you're OK I will go home now, Frau Callighan," said Herr Stein as he started to move towards the door.

I said I could manage, and that I was relieved to know they were no longer in the house. But when he was gone, I felt terrible. With wobbly legs I checked the safe, which was built in our basement; fortunately its contents were all there. In the kitchen, which the thieves apparently had not visited, I made myself a cup of tea in an attempt to calm down and then finally called the police.

***

Exhausted, I sank in a chair once the police was gone. I had barricaded the door so that I would be safe tonight. Herr Stein had promised to replace the lock tomorrow. The police had taken photographs and even checked the drawers of my desk for fingerprints (there were none). I was asked to visit the police station tomorrow to make a formal complaint against unknown, a formality needed for the insurance, although I had little hope they would reimburse the damage. I had called Robert to inform him of the theft, and had reassured him nothing else had been stolen but my laptop. Now, finally, I had time to think about the damage. The police had speculated that the thief or thieves were probably minor criminals, looking for booty that would be easy to sell. They had probably been disturbed, or else they would have continued their search for money, jewellery and such. I had had my phone, purse and driving license with me in my handbag, and my passport had been in the safe, together with other important papers and a few valuable gold items. The thieves had left our antique and arts objects untouched – they probably didn't know the value of those, and even if they did, they would consider the items difficult to sell.

The only thing they had taken was my Mac notebook. That would make a few hundred Euros on the black market. Two things occupied my mind: which data had I lost that I hadn't made a backup of, and could it be this was not an opportunistic theft, in contrast to what the police supposed? I couldn't help but think that there was a connection with the investigations I had recently carried out. That idea really scared me. Who was my enemy? How did he know I was hunting him? What did he need my computer for? And what would have happened in case I had been home?

I hardly slept that night, panicking at every sound.

***

For the first time in weeks I had been really happy for Robert to return home. He had rearranged his Switzerland trip to come home two days earlier than originally planned, worried and anxious to see I was all right. His concerns at first felt like a warm bath and I was glad I didn't have to spend the nights alone at home, so shortly after the burglary, but the pleasure didn't last very long. Robert couldn't stop himself from remarking that we should have repaired that lock weeks ago, and he nearly went as far as to blame me, at least he made it clear it was my own fault my computer was gone. It didn't take long before we were having a row again. My nerves were tight anyway, and I could have done without his hints of accusations. It was obvious that our rough times weren't over yet.

On top of that misery the loss of my computer felt as if a limb was missing. My last backup had been two weeks ago, and fortunately two days ago I had printed some parts of the book chapters I had worked on since that last backup. It meant I'd have to retype those parts that were new, but at least the texts were not lost. Using Robert's computer I saved all chapters from the backup drive in Rich Text Format, so that the files could be opened in a previous version of Word.

From the attic I had recovered my old Macintosh computer, a desktop that still ran on OS9, now a very outdated operating system. Although it had stood collecting dust for a number of years, once plugged in it started up without a glitch. Its opening chord sounded like a voice from the past that brought back pleasant memories. The reason I had replaced it was not because it had been malfunctioning. Rather, most of the software I needed for my work required updates that were no longer compatible with this operating system. Once every five years or so one is forced to update, because everybody else does, though I always feel very uncomfortable with a new computer. It requires so much getting used to, and I am a person of habits. A new computer is like driving a car with manual transmission when you're used to automatic. And once you own a new computer, with a new operating system, you discover the periphery of scanner, printer and the like are no longer compatible, so you have to replace those as well. One update causes another, and I hate such events. Now that I viewed my old, familiar desktop again, I felt like a time traveller visiting the past. My mind tuned into the patterns of routine of those days which my memory had not wiped out yet; I still remembered how to open programmes or where certain menus were located. It was like skating, or riding a bicycle: once you've learned the skill, you won't forget.

I set the date and time and checked what files were still stored on the hard disk of old 'Maccie'. Oh yes, those were the projects I had been working on, those were the days! I connected the external drive with the RTF files and copied everything into a new folder on the desktop. Starting up Word, I prayed this would work. It would take several weeks to come to an agreement with my insurance company, and I didn't want to buy a new computer before I knew whether they were going to reimburse anything. Sure enough the chapters opened from the RTF-files. I saved them as Word files, knowing that upgrading them to a newer version of the text-processing programme wouldn't be a problem, once I had bought a new computer. At least I could continue my work!

Getting the Internet connection to work took a little bit longer, but eventually, by use of an Ethernet cable, my good old Maccie was connected to the virtual world again. My missing limb had been temporarily replaced by a prosthesis.

# XV

Collecting the paperwork needed for the insurance was cumbersome. I had called them a number of times, but without a complete file they would not tell me whether the loss would be covered. Expecting that all my efforts would be in vain didn't make it easier to provide them with all the information they needed to take a decision. It included a visit to the police station, as well as help from our friend Tom, who had a copy of the invoice that listed the serial number of my stolen laptop (my administration was in such a poor shape that I had not been able to find that information). He also offered to come over and update a few things on my old desktop, and to bring an old printer along so that I could print (a driver for my recently-bought laser printer was no longer available for OS9).

By and by I tried to restore my daily routine. I missed my recent email correspondence, although they were stored in my smartphone (maybe Tom knew how to connect this to my computer? I should ask him). The browser I was forced to use was so out-of-date that a number of websites didn't show properly, and I missed a number of files that for some reason had not been included on the backup drive. But all in all, I was able to work. Jonathan, my eldest son, had offered help: he could get hold of a second-hand Mac notebook for a small price at eBay. I politely declined, commenting that it were possibly a stolen one, and could he please keep a lookout as my own notebook would probably end up on that website soon.

After informing a few regular clients about the mishap, and apologizing in advance for the delay in some of the ongoing projects, I decided to try getting hold of Dornfeld again. This time, the journalist answered my call first time I tried – most of the times he seemed to be easier to reach than his colleague Schramm.

"Do you have any news about the murders?" he asked without wasting time for politeness.

"I'm working on it, and it looks like there is progress, but I need to double-check a few things. For this I need to know when exactly you received that anonymous letter. I know your story was published on January 28th. Did you receive the letter shortly before that date?"

He hesitated in answering. Or was he trying to remember the date?

"I didn't immediately publish my story. You know, I needed time to check the whereabouts of Bamberg. And there was the winter break. But if it is of any help to you, I received that letter before Christmas. Why could that be important?"

"Could you be more exact, Herr Dornfeld? Can you recall the date? Maybe you can check on the postal stamp of the envelope?"

"Sorry, I didn't keep the envelope. It bore a local post stamp, I remember that, but since it didn't mention a sender I didn't see a reason why I should keep it."

I had to revive his memory. This was potentially important!

"Please think about it. The murder took place on December the fourth. *Heiligabend* was on a Thursday. Did you receive the letter shortly after the murder, or closer to Christmas?"

"It was a couple of days before Christmas, I think."

If he had received that letter before Christmas, why was his article published more than a month later? I guess he hadn't worked over the Christmas holidays. But I needed to know the date more precisely.

"Can you recall the day of the week? Maybe you can connect the memory of receiving or opening that letter with something else that happened on that day?"

He was again silent, presumably thinking hard.

"It was the day of my weekly cards night. So it must have been a Thursday."

Playing cards, was he? I guessed that would more likely be poker than bridge, with lots of booze. So it had been a Thursday, *a couple of days before Christmas*. This was explicit enough.

"Thank you, that is most helpful. I'll call you back in a few days' time to report my progress, I promise!" and I hung up before he could say or ask anything more.

This was an appropriate moment to contact Steffan.

***

It had been my idea to have dinner together, and I had suggested my favourite Italian restaurant in town, *Albergo da Giovanni*. The place was run by Italians (in contrast to many Italian restaurants in Germany, where the waiter would not speak more Italian than '*Buona sera*' and the cook would most likely be Turkish or Lebanese) and the food was excellent. Steffan and I met at seven. I had been here so often that Giovanni, the owner, who took a pride to greet all visitors personally, knew me, though he was never quite sure what company I would bring. Sometimes Robert and I had dinner here, and in the old days we had often taken the boys with us.

Since Robert travelled a lot, I had also frequently dined here with the boys but without their father, and sometimes a friend of them came along as well. Because parking was problematic, the driver of our party (either Robert or one of the boys) used to drop me first and then park further down the road, to join me a bit later, so Giovanni always asked me with a quizzed look: '*quanti siete?*', not sure how many people accompanied me this time. Since I had taken various colleagues here on occasions, Giovanni had seen me dine with quite a few different men, and he was not surprised that tonight I appeared with a new dinner partner. God knows what he thought of me!

For the occasion I had chosen to wear a dress, which I don't often do. I hoped Steffan would notice, though he shouldn't think I had made an effort. (He didn't make a comment about my looks, and he was wearing an unpretentious sweater and jeans himself. Maybe that was just as well.) After we had ordered the food (a green salad and *gnocchi al gorgonzola* for me, and *carpaccio* followed by *fettuccine al salmone* for Steffan) and our wine had been brought, Steffan asked about the theft which he'd heard about. I told him that the only thing missing was my computer, and that I was a bit worried about that.

"I know a notebook is a good loot, but isn't it strange that they hadn't searched for money or jewellery? They had opened the drawers in my study, and strewn some papers around, and yet nothing else but my Mac was missing. What do you make of that?"

He was careful about giving an opinion. Theft was not his speciality. But there could be various reasons why nothing else had been taken. Maybe the thief had been disturbed, or he was specialized in trading laptops. That was not unheard of.

"I just keep thinking this has something to do with our investigations," I couldn't help saying.

"That is highly unlikely," was all he would say about it.

"Talking about our investigations, I have news for you." I changed the subject, eager to tell him what I had found out.

"Remember my theory about Kazinski being the potential author of those anonymous letters?"

"It was your theory 2, if I recall, and he would blackmail that politician." His memory was excellent!

"Indeed. But listen to this. Kazinski received the results of those hair fingerprints on Friday December 18th. The technician who had performed the experiments remembered which day exactly she reported the results to her boss. The first anonymous letter, however, was received by that journalist, Dornfeld, on Thursday, one day before Kazinski even knew about the fingerprints. So that rules him out as the author of that letter."

I tried not to sound triumphant, but I was proud of myself that I had worked that out. Dornfeld had said it was a Thursday, and a few days before Christmas. That ruled out Christmas Eve (which the Germans include in their definition of Christmas) so at the latest it would have been Thursday 17th. That statement from Dornfeld had cleared Kazinski.

Steffan nodded, which I had learned he always did when he received novel information.

"I also recall that your theory number 3 was that Kazinski was both the murderer and the author of the letters, so that possibility is now also dismissed, isn't it?" Now it was my time to nod.

"That leaves the murderer as the author of those letters, and it isn't Kazinski." This time he said it with triumph in his voice. He had not believed the head of the forensic lab was involved in this anyway.

"But it doesn't rule out blackmail," I said, without getting a reply, as Giovanni brought our starters.

We ate in silence for a while, until I asked what his group had found out about the murder cases. I didn't want to push him further on potential blackmailing activities of Kazinski; time would tell whether I was right or not.

It turned out they had found two possible connections between the two victims.

"The two women were members of the same health club. I'm personally not convinced this is a lead, but we'll follow up on it."

"What is the name of that club?" I was curious to know. Maybe they visited the same gym as I did, which after all was a woman-friendly health centre. But the name he mentioned was that of a different gym.

"And what about the other clue?" I asked. Now he became enthusiastic. He tempered his voice slightly.

"That is far more interesting, in my opinion. Both ladies participated in various chat groups, related with their profession. Some of those chat sessions stored on their computers were encrypted, and our IT specialists are working on them. It turns out they are hard to decipher, but we already know that they use the same kind of encryption. And that may not be a coincidence."

"What exactly does that mean? Did the two women participate in the same chat room?"

"No, there was no direct connection, as far as we can tell. But two independent chat rooms used the same encryption methodology. What if a hacker broke into both? Or if the organisation behind those chat rooms is one and the same? Many of these online enterprises are post box companies, which are often connected some way or another, and oftentimes they are involved in criminal activities as well. And why do these chats have to be encrypted in the first place? Those are the questions we're currently concentrating on."

Steffan seemed convinced this was an important lead. I complemented him with the breakthrough, if that was what it was. I didn't let him sense that I had reservations about this lead. Instead, I changed the conversation away from his job, and asked how his daughter was doing. Melanie had chosen to become a hotelier, and was now being trained in a rather famous hotel in Berlin. She thoroughly enjoyed it, according to her proud father, but they made her work very hard.

"So that means your wife and you are childless again?" I couldn't remember if Melanie had younger siblings.

"Margareta and I separated a year ago. So it's just me now," was his reply, in his neutral, matter-of-fact manner.

"I'm sorry to hear that."

What could I say?

I didn't know his wife that well, and I didn't want to know more details. A man who turns single after being married for so long can be a threat to a woman whose marriage is going through a rough phase, especially if he is as attractive as this one. I did my best to keep the conversation neutral, while steering away from private affairs. When the dinner was finished and coffee with grappa had been consumed, it was time to go home. We parted as friends, and I was kind of relieved that there was no tension in the air. *Better not make things more complicated, Sue!*

# XVI

Steffan had mentioned the computer encryption as a lead he considered promising. By coincidence, I had also considered following up on a computer clue, but in a different direction. I considered asking our whiz kid Tom whether he had contacts in the hacker scene. I'd love to know if there was an extended DNA fingerprint database hidden in the computer system of Kazinski's lab.

Tom was a person with a history. He had been a highly talented, highly gifted young boy. His parents, who we counted amongst our friends since our early days in Germany, had done everything to keep his little brain busy, but he was so intelligent and bright that he skipped class at school twice and was still bored. He was barely sixteen when he was ready to enter university, which he wanted to do by combining two studies: physics and informatics. Everybody told him this would be madness, and since only one university would allow this combination, he left home and lived in a distant city. Despite his young age, for a year he seemed to be doing fine. But during his second year at university, he changed. A wrong choice of friends, too much freedom, too young to realize the consequences of his actions… he started to drink, do drugs, and skip lectures. Soon he got himself into trouble. His studies came to a halt with an arrest for hacking activities.

His parents tried their best, but there was little they could do. I remember his father came over to us one night to talk about his worries. Tom would turn eighteen in a few months, the age by which he would be allowed by law to take decisions for himself. It would reduce the influence of the parents even more, although they would still have to financially support him.

His parents didn't let him down despite his wrongdoings and eventually were able to convince him to return to a normal life. Tom had a lucky escape: in a moment of clarity he realized that he was throwing his life away and he agreed to come home, after a stay in a detox clinic. He lived with them for a year, during which he started a business in computer assistance; this was how we became his customer. After that year he felt ready to continue his studies, this time concentrating on informatics only, and registered at our local university. Ever since he had done just fine. He kept his business running in the background, passing every exam seemingly without an effort. He was close to graduation now, after which he planned to expand his company.

With his background, hacking a computer at the Forensic Institute would not be difficult for Tom, but it would put him in a vulnerable position. He had come clear of his past, and I didn't want to put him off track again. Moreover, when I reflected on this some more, I considered it unlikely such a database would be stored on, or accessible from a computer that was connected to the Internet. The safest protection against hackers is to keep a computer on which sensitive information resides disconnected from the virtual world. Kazinski was intelligent enough to know this. And, besides, I had already been involved in enough illegal activities. So I thought it better not to follow up on this.

Instead, I checked, on the web, for information about the health club that Steffan had mentioned. Its name was '*In Corpore Sano*' which I thought was an appropriate name for a fitness club. Strangely enough, though, I couldn't find it on the web; the club didn't seem to have a website, and their telephone number was neither listed in the directory nor in the Yellow Pages. I sent an email to Steffan to ask for the address of *In Corpore Sano*.

But before I could investigate any further, I was overtaken by the events of the next day.

***

The turmoil started when I opened my morning newspaper. On the front page more details about the prostitute murder cases were presented. I couldn't believe what was printed there, black on white! The story mentioned hairs that had been found on the victims, black hairs on that of Lena and blond hairs on the body of Laila. Moreover, there had been remains of latex detected on both bodies. The police now investigated the connection between these two cases, or so the story said.

I felt my stomach contract. How the hell could the newspaper know this? The author of the item was not released, but I could only think of Dornfeld: he had not kept his promise of a week's moratorium. My anger rose by the minute while I considered what to do, until my telephone rang.

It was Dornfeld. And he was as angry as I was.

He blamed me of foul play: I had released information to another journalist while forbidding him to publish. He was rude and angry and wouldn't take a breath to give me a chance to interrupt his insults, while he shouted at the top of his voice in the telephone. Eventually, though, he paused to take a deep breath and I could reply.

"You're mistaken. I have not released that information to the press, I can assure you! I actually thought you were the author of that article!" He snorted, commenting there was information in there that he didn't know.

"You never said anything about latex, did you? So how could I know that, *bitteschön*?" Of course he had not written it. But now that I had broken my word he would... Rudely I interrupted his threats.

"I repeat myself, I have not broken my promise! I can't explain how this information got to the press. Unless..." a thought just struck my mind. The information presented in that news item had all been collected in one small table that had been stored on my laptop!

"Herr Dornfeld, it is possible the source of that information was a stolen laptop. There has been a burglary in my house a few days ago, and my laptop was taken. I hadn't stored much about these murder cases on my computer, but what you read in today's newspaper is exactly the data I had summarized in a table that was saved on my hard disk." I had known all along that that theft had not been a coincidence!

"I still feel like I've been used!" was his stubborn answer.

"Look, there are other people being harmed far more severely by this article. I have to get in touch with certain persons. I'll call you back before noon to let you know if you can take revenge and publish the blackmail theory. All right?" I needed to pacify him quickly. Right now, all I could think of was to contact Steffan. He would not be pleased with this news!

Dornfeld agreed to wait a few hours, though he threatened that, if he didn't hear from me before twelve o'clock, he would take his own decisions.

With a sigh I disconnected the journalist and called Steffan next.

***

"Yes, I have seen the article," was his cold reply. Steffan was clearly of the opinion that I had leaked to the press. I hastened to correct him, and told him about the table on the stolen laptop. At least this cleared my conscience about the information I had released to Dornfeld last week, in exchange for him telling me about the anonymous letter. All of that was now overrun by the article of today. Steffan never had to know about my 'negotiations' with the press. At this very moment not I, but he was in trouble.

"Sue, even if you're right, and the newspaper got this from your laptop," from his intonation I could gather he wasn't convinced this was what had happened, "the next question that will be asked is, how did that sensitive information got saved on your laptop? You know very well that I should not have released that data to you." Yes, I had realized. He was now the scapegoat.

"Steffan, I'm terribly sorry that I stored that information on my computer. I know I shouldn't have done so. But consider the odds. Who would have stolen my computer by coincidence, get past my password protection, to find a table amongst thousand of files that were pretty much incomprehensible" (he had seen a print of it himself) "and nevertheless know what it meant, and went to the press with it. That is highly unlikely, isn't it?"

"Well, it happened," he said dryly and in a bad mood.

"Or this didn't quite happen by chance. Maybe my computer was stolen for exactly that reason: to find out what I knew about the cases. A commissioned theft, isn't that more what this looks like?"

"And who would know you were investigating these cases?" he asked with a sharp undertone in his voice.

There were two people who knew, and both worked for the press: Dornfeld and Schramm. The first had just yelled at me that he felt used, excluding him from being the thief. But what about Schramm?

"Steffan, I told you I had spoken to both journalists who had received those anonymous letters. Both knew that I was investigating these cases. The guy Dornfeld who had published the Bamberg connection has already called me this morning, shouting with anger. He has nothing to do with today's story. I'm not so sure the other one, Schramm, is also innocent."

Silence on the other end of the line.

"I'm not saying Schramm has broken into my house, but he could have commissioned someone. You know journalists often have ties with the underworld, and they often get away with it because their sources are protected."

"I think I'll ask my people to pay a visit to that Herr Schramm," he sounded tense.

It was not easy to interfere with the press. A journalist would immediately cry out about *Pressefreiheit*, freedom of the press. But if Schramm's story could be connected to a stolen computer, he could be accused of fencing, in combination to obstruction of police investigations. Schramm would soon be in trouble, I was sure about that.

I thanked Steffan for taking the trouble to check this, and promised him I would let him know if I had any further news.

Keeping my word, before noon I called Dornfeld back and suggested he present the story about Kazinski faking forensic evidence. Whether or not he would mention blackmail was up to him. I had not found evidence for that theory, and that's what I told him, but he seemed to fancy speculative stories. Whatever he was going to write, Kazinski's reputation would be damaged, and I no longer cared that I could be traced as the source of that story. Now that my surrogate brain, my hard disk, was available to the press, I might as well release a darker side of my real mind to the newspaper.

***

That night, I reproduced the table from memory. Was there anything else that the press could deduce from it? It was highly unlikely that they would extrapolate the information to forecast a third murder the way I had tried to. And, besides, my prediction had been wrong. I had not been able to predict the date of a third murder. Maybe there would not be another one. Staring at the table once more, now visible on the monitor connected to my old desktop computer, I suddenly realized that I had overseen a possibility last time I thought about this. A third murder that would produce one hair, could also take place on the fourth of April. Four divided by four gives one. That would be in two weeks from now.

# XVII

The circles were definitely expanding, even without a third murder. When Bamberg had been accused of being involved with the first prostitute victim, he had tried to defend himself while pleading innocent, and his insecurity had made his case worse. The recording of the politician stammering in the camera in lack of words to prove his innocence had been repeated over and over on TV. Florian Helmuth, the captain of industry, was cut out of different wood. His response to the recent accusations that he had liaised with the second victim was aggressive rather than defensive. He never publicly denied he had known the woman, but instead hired a bunch of expensive lawyers to charge anybody with libel who dared repeat what the press had written. No doubt Thomas Schramm and his newsagent had also received a letter from his lawyers. In the meantime, the public savoured the drama; this was real entertainment!

With this level of excitement going on, the publication of presumed falsification of forensic data in relation to these crimes caused an uproar in the press. Dornfeld had been clever enough to publish this new item under a pseudonym. The effect wasn't any less. Kazinski was asked for a reaction in front of the cameras, which he stubbornly refused. His round, dwarf-like face was all over the papers. Chief Inspector Braun referred to the sensitivity of information that could hamper ongoing police investigations and would not say more, but from his expression I could tell a storm was brewing and he knew he would be in it soon. Bamberg the politician insisted on forming a committee to investigate the allegations against the Forensic Institute of presumable manipulation of forensic evidence. Experts and self-named experts fought for attention in discussion programmes to comment how this could have happened, and what the consequences could be. In view of the typical German fear for loss of privacy, and a widespread mistrust towards everything that had to do with DNA in general, the discussion was broadened until it had little to do with the original fraud. At one stage I was asked to participate in a panel discussion on the local television, which I naturally declined. I felt little need to get publicly involved in this.

Steffan Braun didn't contact me to let me know what he thought of my latest move. I suspected he knew I was behind this defamation of Kazinski, although he couldn't rule out that the charging information had been stored on my computer as well, and that it had found its way into the open via that route. I decided to lay low for a while, and promised myself to only contact him if I could provide him with real, valuable, novel facts. Facts that could aid in solving these murders, and clear his name and reputation.

***

That Tuesday afternoon I was on my way home from a visit to the headquarters of my bank. I had arranged an appointment to evaluate our assets with our financial manager. I wanted to know what my financial situation was, so that I would be prepared if things turned bad with respect to my marriage. Right now life with Robert seemed to continue as if nothing had happened, but I didn't know what the near future would have in stock for me. And in any case, it didn't hurt to go through the paperwork with an expert and take action with a few investments that could be improved. I had dressed up for the occasion. The weather was typical for March: sunshine one moment and rain or a snowstorm next. A winter coat was still needed, but under it I wore a blazer matching a tight skirt and high heels. With my hair tied up in a bun and a briefcase under my arm I looked like one of these female investment bankers that populated the streets of Frankfurt, the financial heart of Germany. The reason to dress up like that was twofold. I felt more secure this way, and I would be treated with more respect by the bank; years of experience had taught me that one's outfit can influence how people react.

On my way home my phone buzzed to announce an incoming mail. It happened to come from Steffan. His email was a response to my request for the address of the health club *In Corpore Sano*. This was a good sign! Apparently, he didn't blame me for the latest press leak; at least, I interpreted his responding email as a sign of trust and credence. It seemed he didn't mind if I investigated further; why else would he have sent me that address? Since the place was not far from where I was, I decided to explore the place right now.

Close to where the address was located I parked my car and walked the last few hundred metres. The presence of a health club wasn't obvious at all. No neon logo on the facade, no pictures of sporty youngsters, not even the beautiful Latin name was shown. The door that bore the street number Steffan had mailed me was made of milky glass set in chrome. There was a letterbox without a name and a doorbell, nothing else. Well, that matched the anonymity of this club on the web. Apparently, they had no need to advertise in order to collect members.

I rang the bell and waited. A buzz indicated the door was being unlocked and I pushed it open. When I entered I smelled a scent of menthol mixed with eucalypt. It was warm in here, so I took off my coat and put it over my arm. At the end of a short corridor was a small reception desk behind which, finally, the name *In Corpore Sano* was displayed in wavy letters. The lady receptionist on duty welcomed me with a lipstick smile. She was in her forties and had an enormous bosom, which was only partly hidden by her open blouse. She wore too much makeup for this time of the day and her jewellery was excessive; she looked more like she was ready to go to the theatre than to work in a health club. The multiple golden rings dangling from her earlobes tinkled as she moved her head. She asked politely what she could do for me. I replied that I was interested in becoming a member of their Club. Still with that fire-red smile on her face, she replied:

"Our club only welcomes new members upon invitation. Who can I put down has invited you?"

So it was this kind of a club. Let's see if I could bluff myself into this. There were two names I could choose from; one of those belonged to a person who had denied everything they wrote about him, so I put my chances on the other.

"My dear friend Florian. Florian Helmuth, of course."

It worked, and the lady didn't seem surprised at all when I mentioned the name of this famous CEO.

"Oh, a man inviting the lady this time, for a change. Why not?"

I wasn't quite sure what she meant with that, but she accepted the invitation and opened a book in front of her to write Helmuth's name down. I wondered how she could hold a pen with those outrageously long fingernails. No computer was to be seen, bureaucracy was based on old-fashioned handwriting here.

"And your name is?"

I didn't know why I should lie about this, so I gave her my real name, which she also wrote down.

"What shall I put down as your profession?" That was a strange question, as I couldn't figure its relevance to joining a fitness club. I had to react quickly. I looked business-like, in these clothes and with a briefcase in my hand. This club was a members-only health club that didn't advertise, and it was visited by CEOs like Helmuth. I decided to remain vague.

"I'm a consultant. Self-employed."

She smiled her lipstick again.

"That's 'personal coach' then?" She let it sound as if the majority of self-employed well-dressed consultants were personal coaches. Slowly I started to feel uncomfortable.

"That will do. May I ask what the fee is?"

She handed me a brochure that she had taken out of a drawer.

"This contains all the information you need. We are open on Tuesday, Thursday, Friday and Saturday nights. Please sign the form at the back and return it with your bank account data next time you visit us. Welcome to our club."

Astonished, I took the leaflet, thanked her and turned on my heels. This was the strangest health club I had ever seen!

***

That afternoon, I called Peter Eichholz. Since that evening I had seen Bamberg on television, pleading for a committee to investigate the presumed misdoings in the Forensic Institute, I had been thinking about this. Now I was sure it was time to act. I told Peter the time was ripe for Bamberg to provide a sample of his DNA to the police, in front of the television. It would suffice more than one purpose. It would show that the politician still had faith in forensic investigations; it would clear him once and for all from the allegations about him and that prostitute, and it would be a signal to Kazinski that Bamberg would not be fooled. If – I was still not certain about this – but if Kazinski was blackmailing Bamberg about a matching DNA fingerprint, this public action would put an end to that. I didn't mention all this to Peter: I only used the argument of faith. But Peter liked the idea of a public statement from his client, and said he would talk to Bamberg tomorrow.

***

Something else was bothering me. I had read the brochure of *In Corpore Sano* from front to back. The photos showed healthy, good-looking young men and women working on exercise machines, but it didn't look as if they were doing a proper workout. The men wore sleeveless T-shirts and tight shorts; the women looked quite sexy in their skin-tight leotards. Instead of sweatbands and ponytails, their hair was worn open and well coiffed, and they all wore makeup. Had these photos been taken using models? A photo of the bar was prominently placed in the middle of the leaflet, portraying men and women enjoying cocktails, still in their sports wear. The club had an extensive wellness area with a sauna (I recalled the smell of menthol mixed with eucalypt, which indeed had reminded me of a sauna). Massages were also offered: a photo showed a middle-aged man being massaged by a pretty girl wearing a minute bikini. There was also a photo of a small swimming pool with four naked bathers. I knew of various public places in Germany where FKK activities were allowed. FKK is the abbreviation for *Freikörperkultur*, naturism. It had been very popular in former Eastern Germany, and after the reunification, FKK activities became gradually more accepted in the Western part of the country as well. Even the local swimming pool in our city was open two hours a week for nude swimmers. Public saunas advised their visitors not to wear bathing suits, and signs warned about this; it can be just as embarrassing entering a sauna in bathing costume where all other guests are naked, as the other way round. (For those who didn't fancy to mix naked with the other gender, most saunas also offered separate male and female evenings). But the way this health club presented their activities was different. This was not a normal fitness centre! Knowing that both murdered prostitutes had been members, after reading this folder I was certain I needed to investigate the place at more detail.

I wondered how long the lipstick lady would need to find out that Florian Helmuth had never invited me, or even knew me. I had to act quickly.

# XVIII

I decided to take action immediately. I would pay a visit to that club this very night. After all, it was Tuesday, one of the four nights per week the club would be open. A visit required some preparation: I needed to blend with the crowd, if I were able to get past the reception desk at all. I had visions of Lady Lipstick clawing her long fingernails in my shoulders to stop me from entering. But if she had not done her homework yet, I'd be able to get in, at least tonight, and in that case I should be one of them. A 'personal coach'.

I didn't own a leotard, at least not of the kind that looked anything like what the folder showed. In my own gym I usually wore a long-sleeved one, with a loose-fitting T-shirt over it, and my tights were hidden in baggy jogging trousers. That would definitely not do for tonight. I dashed into town to visit a sports garment shop. They didn't have what I was looking for. I ended up buying something in a shop next to the cinema, a shop of a kind I had never entered before. Suffice to say that there were vibrators on display on top of the counter.

***

I was nervous when I left the house that night. Under my normal sports clothes I wore a black leotard that had a low-cut back. My leggings were black, too, with a white line running from my heels all the way up (which was really all the way up, as the body had a tanga cut). I felt slightly ridiculous with this outfit, though, in all fairness, I didn't have to be ashamed of my body. I could lie ten years off my age, and I could imagine certain men with a MILF preference would fancy me (whether I liked those men was another question). I had tied my hair in a bun on top of my head, which made my cheekbones come out, and had put on evening makeup, which I normally wouldn't wear when going for a workout.

Fortunately, Robert hadn't noticed: he had not come home that night, falling back to his pattern of unfaithful husband again. I would deal with that later.

I had filled out the form at the back of the brochure, and was prepared to pay the monthly fee of one hundred and fifty Euros, at least for one month. It was far too expensive for a health club, and I just hoped the investment would be worth it. I wasn't quite sure what to expect from this night, though. In order to be prepared for the worst I had armed myself: in my drinking bottle, which had a wide opening and was made of non-transparent plastic, a can of pepper spray was hidden.

With trembling fingers I pressed the same doorbell I had pressed earlier today and waited for the door-opening buzz. A different lady was working at the reception tonight, a younger and prettier version of Lady Lipstick. I handed her the form and she welcomed me with a smile, while she glanced over the piece of paper to check my name:

"Your first night here? Welcome... Sue." She took my name down in her book and checked that I had filled out the payment form completely. Then she explained that the ladies' changing room was to the right. I took a deep breath and went in.

It turned out not to be as bad as I had feared. Two ladies were chatting in the changing room while they took off their coats. They greeted me with a friendly nod. I slowly stripped off my outer layer of sportswear, ensuring that I would be ready when they were, so that I could follow them. They took their time to prepare themselves, while I pretended to improve my makeup. Their garments were even more daring than mine; at least my choice of style had been correct. Eventually, they made a move and I hurried behind their swaying hips, with my towel and my water bottle under my arm. The latter I had filled with cotton wool to avoid the pepper spray can from clonking. The two ladies walked through the corridor to the fitness studio, where they mounted their bikes next to each other. I chose a stepper a little behind them. They slowly started spinning and I programmed my machine for an easy climb. This was not the place to work yourself into a sweat.

While I was calmly stepping, I watched my surroundings. The workout room was not particularly big, but larger than most of the fitness rooms I had visited in hotels. Easy listening music played in the background. There were six women present (not counting myself); one was doing stretching exercises on a mat, the others worked the machines. It seemed they were really doing exercises, though not over-exerting themselves. Five men were also present. They were less occupied with their workout, although one was lifting weights to show off his muscles. The men mostly sat at ease on the machines, not moving any weights, or they walked around, eying the ladies without reservation. Even I received a few inquisitive looks.

After fifteen minutes I decided to go to the bar. I couldn't drink from my water bottle (I noticed I was the only one carrying one) and my mouth was dry, more from being nervous than from exertion. A sign showed me the way.

The bar was dimly lit and soft jazz was played here. A few couples were seated at the bar. Nobody used the comfortable couches placed along the walls. I ordered a mineral water and added hastily, after noticing the quizzical look from the barman, a martini as well. It didn't take long before company presented itself. One of the men who had observed me in the gym approached me and, with a nod, seated himself to my right.

"Hi, I haven't seen your pretty face here before, you're new?" His opening line was rather dull.

"New in town!" I lied. Smalltalk followed. My English accent drew his interest, or so he pretended. I noticed his eyes were fixed on my breasts, although my towel hung over my shoulders in a vain attempt to cover the deep cut of my garment. I felt vulnerable in this crazy outfit. It wouldn't take long before a hand would place itself on my thigh. *Sue, why the hell did you go here?*

"I would like to know you a little better, *Schatz,*" the guy, who had introduced himself as Frank, moved a bit closer. His eau de toilette was heavy and musky. Not my taste. And he wasn't my type, either. His eyes were set too wide apart in his face, and his lips were very thin, which gave his face a mean expression. His body was not in a bad shape, I had to admit, but he was not the sort of man I would fancy.

"The evening is still young…" I replied in an attempt to slow him down.

"I understand. Looking for more than one customer, are you?" he asked hornily. So that was how it worked. Men met women, merchandise was being tested and an arrangement was made. The rest of the trade was probably consumed in her apartment. It might actually work better than selecting a woman from a website presenting pictures only. The barman (who, with his stature of a bodybuilder, was probably the only person in this room who really used the fitness machines seriously) provided some protection for the girls against over-enthusiastic customers.

"I usually take my time. But if you leave me your number, I'll contact you when I'm ready." I needed to be in control! He took the bait and wrote a number down on a piece of paper that the barman had helpfully handed him.

"Only call me on Wednesdays between seven and eight in the evening, OK?" So he was married and that hour of the week his wife would not be home. Nice to know. "And don't keep me waiting forever, will you?" he added. I was glad he wasn't too persistent.

I smiled at him with a sweet but not too inviting smile as I took the number and hopped off my seat, leaving half of my martini behind. I was stopped halfway by Lady-Lipstick-the-Elder, who had appeared from nowhere. With a stern look on her face she begged me to follow her. I realized my cover had been blown and expected she would direct me towards the exit. I was wrong. She led me to the first floor, where we entered a small office. She took her place behind a desk and pointed at the only other chair, indicating I was supposed to take a seat as well. Without much of an introduction she started off:

"My name is Esmeralda but everybody calls me *Mutti*. I am going to explain our house rules to you." In a business-like manner she talked me through the rules. She had no restraint to describe the practice of this club. She persistently called the female members 'girls', who were supposed to arrange meetings with the men, with every appointment to be reported to Carlo the barkeeper. For every meeting the club would receive fifty Euros, to be paid by the girl. Using one of the in-house rooms cost twenty Euros per hour. There was a minimum of six appointments per month to be arranged. Breaking that rule would cost three hundred Euros in addition to the monthly fee. Breaking the rule for a period longer than three months meant the membership would be cancelled. A medical check-up would be provided on a monthly basis and this was compulsory, to be paid by the girl. Appointments made with the men without notifying the club were forbidden and would be punished by immediate exclusion from the club. Every girl was supposed to introduce a new female member at least once every two months. Open drunkenness and the use of drugs were forbidden. And so it went on and on.

I sat there, listening to this introduction into a world I had only vaguely known existed. These girls were obviously being exploited by the club, being forced to produce a minimum turnover and paying for extra expenses out of their income from their prostitution activities. They had to ensure new flesh would enter the club on a regular basis to satisfy the needs of the male customers. What was the advantage for them to agree to these terms? I guess it was the protection they received from Carlo, plus the certainty of meeting wealthy customers. I wondered how much the membership cost for the men, but I didn't dare to ask. Mutti was not the type to answer enquiring questions. However, it was certain that the club would earn a fortune with this business, without having to do or to risk very much.

The rules also explained a few things: why Mutti had expressed surprise that my introducer was male, for instance, or why they didn't advertise. Or why the two murdered prostitutes had used encrypted websites to offer their services independently from the club, which they weren't allowed to do.

I quickly did my calculations. In addition to the hundred and fifty Euros I had to pay as a monthly fee, I would have to pay for the medical check up, which was to take place as soon as possible, plus the punishment of three hundred Euros in case I didn't produce the required turnover. This was going to become an expensive endeavour! But with my knowledge it shouldn't be too difficult for Steffan to investigate the books that Carlo kept, in order to identify customers that Laila and Lena had shared. I might never have to return to this terrible place: I had seen enough to present the police with a nice lead.

'Mutti' Esmeralda (unlikely this was her real name) had finished her sermon and had produced another form that I had to fill in and sign, to confirm I accepted their rules. With that, the session was over.

I felt a slight nausea when I descended the stairs. I had expected this club to be a meeting point for sex workers, but I had not been prepared for this highly organized slavery. I decided to leave there and then.

As I left I took a last glance at the bar, where to my surprise I discovered a new costumer who looked familiar. I stopped for a moment to make sure. The man in question was in conversation with a woman in a pink outfit and didn't notice me. That was lucky for both of us. We had been colleagues, once, and we would both be terribly embarrassed if an encounter took place. Well, well, the world is full of surprises! What was a molecular biologist working in the Forensic Institute doing in a place like this? Looking for female company, apparently.

***

That night I had learned a lot. *In Corpore Sano*, that had been visited by both murdered prostitutes, was a sex club disguised as a health club. They had probably met their killer here. The arrangements between male and female members were recorded minutely. Florian Helmuth was a member, and possibly Reiner Bamberg was as well – which would explain why the killer had chosen his name to leak to the press after the first murder. I recalled how certain Peter Eichholz had been that his client had never had anything to do with prostitutes. Lies and politics are never far apart! The information I had obtained would please Steffan. But was it enough? It was still possible that Lena and Laila had kept the arranged meeting with their killer out of Carlo's books. In fact, it was quite likely they had, because only then did the murderer feel safe enough to do his thing. Come to think of it, it wouldn't help at all if Steffan and his team interfered at this stage. There were possibly hundreds of male members who visited, or had visited, this club. How to identify the killer amongst them? I decided I needed more time. My membership shouldn't be blown by Helmuth denying he had invited me. Not yet. I had to remain a member and play my role. If needed I even had to meet with customers. That would pay Robert back! Whether I had the nerve to do so was another question, but at least I planned for it. There was no other option than to contact the CEO to ensure my cover.

That Helmuth's secretary would shield her boss off from the outside world was no surprise. He was busy, he was in a meeting, he was travelling, it didn't matter what excuse she used; I knew she was instructed not to put anyone through that couldn't be trusted. Certainly not after all this negative publicity. Eventually I had to use a threat to break through the barrier. I told her that, if she didn't let me speak to her boss, I had no the other option than to contact the police, and that could have severe consequences for Herr Helmuth, who would not be pleased if he found out all of this could have been avoided if his secretary had been a bit more cooperative. It worked.

"*Ja bitte!*" the CEO responded in a demanding tone after I had been put through. I recognized his sharp voice from the television.

"Herr Helmuth, my name is Dr. Sue Swanson. I am a research consultant. We don't know each other but we need to talk. It is about *In Corpore Sano*. Please give me a minute of your time, and be assured that I am on your side."

"Just a moment," was his reply, in a business-like tone, and I heard a click in the line. I guess he switched the call to another extension, or else disconnected his secretary so she could no longer hear what we discussed.

"Explain?" he asked when he was back in the line. He didn't waste time, and it seemed he wanted to get through this unpleasant conversation as quickly as possible.

"I joined that club yesterday by mentioning your name. I pretended to be your invitee, and I would appreciate if you backed me. I believe this club is the key to the recent murder cases, in which your name unfortunately has been mentioned."

"You know I have nothing to do with that and I warn you to be careful what you say! What is your intention?" He asked it with mistrust in his voice.

"I'm investigating those murder cases on my own account. I am specialized in forensic evidence and I have reason to believe there have been mistakes, or rather manipulations, with the evidence presented in relation to these cases."

"I read the newspaper, too. You're not telling me anything that hasn't been published." His mistrust was now obvious.

"I know, but I have more information than was released in the press. I believe there is a connection to *In Corpore Sano,* both to the two victims, and to you and Mr. Bamberg."

"Why do you think I am a member of that club?"

"As I said, I know there is a connection, and when I mentioned you as the person who invited me, it was accepted, which proved your membership. I also know both Lena and Laila, the two murdered women, had been members of the club. I suspect Bamberg is, or was, visiting the place, too. I believe your membership was the reason behind the accusations that you unfortunately have experienced lately. I'm not interested to know if there was any truth in those or not, as that is none of my business. But I need more time to investigate what happens in that club, as I believe the key to identify the murderer can be found there. And to allow me to investigate further, I need your support. Can I count on that?" I was asking a lot. He didn't know me, wouldn't know if he could trust me, and I had nothing to offer in return. I crossed my fingers.

"What did you say your profession was?" Did he ask me this because I had to state my profession at the front desk of the health club, or was he asking for my credentials? I decided to answer the question for both.

"For reasons of my investigation, I pretended to be what club members call a personal coach. In reality I am a researcher. You can check my website if you wish." I gave him the web address.

"You can imagine I don't want anything to do with that club anymore. I was going to cancel my membership next..." I interrupted him:

"Please, give me two weeks. I hope I don't need more time than that." In fact, I hoped I needed less time. I would have to identify the murder before April fourth, if I wanted to avoid a third murder. That was less than a fortnight away. After a pause he said:

"Let me state my conditions to your strange proposal clearly: you never call me at work again. You don't contact me by phone at all, but I will send you an email through your website, to which you may respond if it is absolutely necessary. I will instruct my lawyers to keep an eye on your activities. And I cancel my membership by the first of May. Is that clear?" I expected he would put a private detective, rather than a lawyer, at my trail, but I could live with that. I had nothing to hide that would harm Florian Helmuth. I accepted his conditions and thanked him for his collaboration, which I assured would not harm him in any way. Relieved, I ended the call. So far so good. I could continue pretending to be a 'personal coach' for the next two weeks, and probably expand my professional career into the field of erotic services.

# XIX

Peter Eichholz had not wasted time in instructing his client Bamberg. That day, the politician was shown on television with his mouth wide open while the inside of his cheek was swabbed for a DNA sample. He then smiled into the camera, declaring he still had faith in forensic investigations, provided they were performed correctly, professionally and with the necessary transparency. Nobody seemed to notice that transparency is not compatible with criminal investigations. Transparency is the buzzword of politics nowadays. Everything should be transparent. We are told we live in a world of glass, and every wall apparently should contain windows, for everybody to observe what is happening behind those walls. Nothing should be kept in the dark, for the good of humankind. The activities of Google, Facebook, Twitter, computer clouds and all these other technological wonders has created a global village, where everybody knows everything about everybody else, and this apparently produces a better world. People give up their privacy voluntarily, sharing with their Facebook 'friends' details of their whereabouts and activities that I wouldn't even share with my closest real friends. Instead of socializing, you now have to be connected with several hundred online friends. Checking their activities and being checked by others is all that matters nowadays. To this purpose, this so-called transparency is presented as a good thing, bringing people together. But that isn't the real world we live in. Many activities need to be kept hidden, whether we like it or not. Some acts are best performed in the dark and some information is better kept confidential. Transparency is not helpful if you try to solve a murder. I had no intention at all to disclose that I was investigating undercover, *Transparenz hin oder her*.

The only person who knew me in my real life as well as in my act as 'personal coach' was potentially Dr. Günther Müller, who I had recognized at the bar of *In Corpore Sano*. Müller had worked as a team leader when I collaborated with a different research group of the Forensic Institute. What had happened with him since? I dug out the crumbled folder of the Forensic Institute once more. The bearded face of Müller was definitely not amongst the team members shown on the photograph. I googled him, but the only hits retrieved were related to his past professional activities. A few Günther Müllers were registered in Facebook, but none of these was the molecular biologist I was looking for. LinkedIn and ResearchGate, the social networks most popular in the scientific world, didn't know him. He seemed to have disappeared from the globe, and yet I had seen him Tuesday night enjoying a drink with a girl in a disguised sex club. I was absolutely certain it had been him. So he was still living in this area. Three entries in the telephone directory for Günther Müller were stated for our city. Maybe Monica could tell me more.

***

As if by telepathy, Monica called me that night. She was worried about the recent revelations by the press. Would her name at some stage turn up? She didn't want to lose her job again! I assured her there was nothing to worry about. I didn't tell her I had been the source behind this story, but she could guess. If, in any case, Dr. Kazinski contacted her, trying to put the blame on her, or even threatened her, I urged her to contact me immediately –I ensured her I would protect her. She was relieved, though not completely convinced that she wouldn't be in the fire line some day. I wasn't completely convinced, either.

Now that I had her on the phone I asked her about *Herr Doktor* Günther Müller. Did she know when he had left the Forensic Institute?

"I have never met him, he had changed to another department by the time I joined the lab. But I know his name. We even used a buffer called 'Müller solution' which had been his recipe – it worked fantastic to elute DNA from paper tissues." I recalled my considerations against writing a cookbook for forensics. See, they all stuck to their own inventions! Monica continued: "*Doktor* Müller had been adored by his team members. Everybody was convinced he would become director of the institute, after the previous director announced his retirement, and they were all anticipating he would become their boss. But then out of the blue Dr. Kazinski got the job. My colleagues told me everybody was disappointed, and Müller left the group in a row. I don't know the details."

That was interesting news. Instead of an internal candidate, someone from outside had gotten the job of Director of the Institute. I could imagine Müller had not been pleased. And since my Internet searches had not revealed a continuation of his professional activities, it could well be that Müller was without a job right now. This Kazinski had been the cause of at least two ruined careers. Given his current situation, I guess Müller wouldn't look forward to meet me, and I wasn't keen on exchanging greetings in *In Corpore Sano* with him, either. I'd better be careful not to meet him there.

***

"I had to use all the influence I could exploit," explained Steffan. We were seated in the same lunchroom where I had met Monica that day in January that got me involved in this crazy turmoil of events. The sun was bathing the hillside in a warm light, as spring had definitely arrived. Although I had chosen the location, our meeting had been initiated by him, for which I was grateful. I had hesitated to contact him, as I wasn't sure how he would react after the shit storm that he had had to endure. It seemed he wasn't blaming me for it. Now he informed me that Schramm, the journalist, had published information from my computer.

"Of course, it was out of the question that I would be granted a *Hausdurchsuchungsbefehl*." A search warrant for a journalist? Very unlikely, and Schramm would not have kept my computer in his bedroom, or in his office.

"So how did you find out?"

"I don't think you want to know," was his mysterious answer. So even Braun used methods that couldn't see the light of day, sometimes. So much for transparency. But I am notoriously inquisitive. And I thought I had the right to know whose dirty hands had touched my baby! So I pushed him for more information.

"Fact is, your computer has been found. Right now, it sits on a shelf in the *Asservatenkammer* together with a bunch of other stolen items that we retrieved from the young man." They had arrested a young adolescent for burglary and my computer had not been the only item his long fingers had taken hold of during his recent criminal activities. My computer was checked for fingerprints and, since Steffan had not completely rejected my suggestion that Schramm had based his publication on information from my computer, he ordered the fingerprints to be compared to those of the journalist. It produced a hit, although the man denied having anything to do with the burglary.

I was very glad to hear that my computer had been retrieved and that it was safe now. Few people would be able to approach my computer where it was now, safely locked away in a heavily guarded place inside the *Presidium*. Eventually, I would get it back, I hoped, though I had to be patient, as it would take time before this piece of evidence for burglary and theft could be handed back to its legal owner.

"That is great. And I have news for you as well!" I told him my findings about the health club. How I had registered using the name of Florian Helmuth. And that the club was a disguised sex club. That they recorded all meetings arranged between male and female members. As was his custom, Steffan let me tell the story without interruption, but I could tell he wasn't approving.

"Sue, you must be out of your mind!" he finally commented, after I had finished my report.

"What you did was irresponsible and potentially dangerous! I don't want you to continue with this. This is not a game, you know," he reproached. I ignored his disapproval.

"Steffan, think of the importance of these findings. This club is one of two common leads between the two prostitutes that we know of. Moreover, it also links the two men who have been accused to be involved by anonymous letters, which we believe were sent by the killer. I bet Bamberg is a member of that club, too. All lines point towards that place; we just need to connect the dots…"

"We can investigate their members…" he suggested it with reluctance.

"And then what? The murderer hasn't got the word 'killer' spelt behind his name, has he? How do you want to identify him? He didn't leave a trace at the crime scenes, remember? He wouldn't be so daft to have the meeting recorded in the club book during which he killed!" and before he could say something, I continued with the other clue I had discovered.

"We don't have much time, Steffan. I think there will be a next murder soon. Remember I had tried to extrapolate the date for a third murder, with the prediction of one hair to be left on the victim? I believe that could happen very soon, on the fourth of April."

He whistled through his teeth in amazement – that was only ten days from now. It wouldn't leave us much time to act. Or was his reaction a sign that he wasn't taking my prophecy seriously?

"I hope you're wrong. In fact, I think it is unlikely one can accurately predict the time of the next murder – if there is to be another." He used just the same intonation as he did when agreeing with my views. With his degree of professionalism, disagreeing with a statement was just as significant as agreeing. There were no personal issues here. I could take criticism. Being a scientist, I was used to people trying to prove me wrong. I asked him for the reasons behind his reservations.

"You deduced this prediction from a mathematical calculation with the dates of two murders, right? I remember you pointed out yourself that the human mind is searching for connections where there aren't any. You are extrapolating two dates in the past with a third, in the future. Now, I am not a mathematician, but I know that two points can be joined by a straight line, as well as by an infinite number of curves. Correct, *Frau Doktor*?" He was slightly ridiculing me now. But he was right, of course. He continued:

"It is highly unlikely that the dates of these murders were planned beforehand, with a schedule leading up to a third murder. More likely, the deeds were performed when the conditions allowed it. There may be a general plan behind the whole thing – the placing of those hairs on the victims suggests so, but I am reluctant to put a meaning in their dates. I won't take that as a fact to predict a third murder. From experience I know such crimes typically happen by a coincidence of factors."

I wasn't going to contradict him. He was the specialist. I skipped to the next bit.

"Let's leave that point for the moment. There have been so many developments lately that the murderer must be getting nervous. I believe we need to put even more pressure on the killer. We need to force him to make mistakes. And I need to be in that club, as I think he will select his next victim from within that circle."

Steffan was silent, not nodding or reacting at all to what I said.

"I think the killer was not pleased with the action by Bamberg to deliver his DNA voluntarily. It was a public statement that he was innocent, and whatever the killer had wanted to achieve with that letter to Dornfeld seems to have come to a halt. I suggest the same strategy would work for Helmuth."

"Hang on, why do you say 'strategy'? Was it you... you didn't tell Bamberg to hand in a DNA sample, did you?" Steffan was slowly recognizing my way of working.

"Let me say I was able to influence his decisions in some way. And I am in touch with Helmuth as well. I think I could convince him to do the same thing Bamberg did. That would irritate the killer, for sure."

Now Steffan started his usual nodding again. I took that for his consent in this matter.

"I think I should try to get an undercover agent inside that club." He was now thinking aloud. I didn't think that was our best option, though.

"But they shouldn't discover that they're being watched! We don't know how much the club's owners are involved in this. They must have realized that the two murder victims were amongst their members, and they must have put two and two together. The fact that they didn't close down their business suggests that either they don't care, or that maybe even the organizers are themselves involved."

"And how do you think you would get any closer to the truth, or discover the identity of the killer, in case you were allowed to investigate further? I repeat, *in case you were...*" Ignoring his suggestion that I needed his permission to investigate, I had my response to this question ready. I had thought about my strategy long before this conversation.

"If my prediction of the date for a third murder is correct, we should have to know of all women who arrange a meeting with a club member on the fourth of April, so that they can get protection. We could even use them as a decoy. What do you think of that?"

This time Steffan wasn't nodding, but shaking his head with determination.

"As I said earlier, you must be out of your mind!" he just remarked. But was my idea so outrageous? I didn't think so.

# XX

My email to Florian Helmuth was sent immediately after he had contacted me from a webmail address. I explained that the recent action of Bamberg to deliver a DNA sample voluntarily had been a public statement of innocence, and I strongly suggested him to do the same, as that would provide positive publicity. I kept my message formal and short – imagining he would normally send and prefer to receive messages that were as concise as possible. Not telling him so, I hoped he would assist in our attempts to make the killer nervous and to stop the circles from expanding any further. We should force the developments into a direction the murderer had not anticipated. Then, maybe, he would make a mistake.

I looked back to the beginning of his actions. The first murder, of poor Lena Lotus, and the three hairs he had left. Black hairs, that he had possibly collected from a public place. Or had he selected them more carefully? Bamberg's hair was black, and the killer could have collected a hair from his clothes in the changing room of *In Corpore Sano*. There had been lockers in the ladies' changing room, but most women had hung their winter coats on hangers in the corner, approachable to anybody. If the same was custom in the gents' changing room as well...Would the killer have selected a black hair from Bamberg on purpose, and mixed it with two hairs from other individuals? Other club members, or strangers... maybe he just added those two other hairs to add complexity, to avoid an early discovery, or to put the police on a false lead. Come to think of it, Helmuth was blond!

I grabbed the phone and dialled Steffan's number. We needed to get in touch with Kazinski, and get him to play straight. It was ridiculous that we couldn't trust the results of the Forensic Institute. The DNA evidence was now crucial, once again! It needed some encouragement from my part to make Steffan see how important this was, but eventually he agreed he would set up a meeting between the three of us. Kazinski would have to come clean of his sins.

***

If you are summoned by the Chief Inspector to appear at the *Presidium*, you'd better be there. I arrived way ahead of the appointment, dressed in a dull work suit that I thought matched the occasion, and was formally greeted by Steffan Braun:

"Good day to you, Frau Dr. Swanson." The formality was required since a junior officer was present as well. Shortly after I had taken a seat in the small conference room, Dr. Gottfried Kazinski entered, slightly overdressed in a dark suit, with waistcoat and tie. He was utterly surprised to see me. Steffan wanted to introduce me, but I was faster:

"*Hallo Doktor* Kazinski, *so sieht man sich wieder*!" A wonderful neutral sentence, this 'so we meet again', that didn't reveal whether I was pleased or not about seeing him again. Steffan explained I was present as an external expert and observer only, we all shook hands, and then took our places around the table.

The next twenty minutes were not easy for Kazinski. Sweat drops appeared on his forehead. He was being accused of withholding forensic evidence, although he was not given an explanation how Braun knew about it. All the Inspector said was that there was 'convincing evidence' that Kazinski's report had been incorrect, and he had been summoned to explain what had gone wrong. Braun described matter-of-factly that 'according to particular information we have received' three DNA fingerprints had been obtained from samples recovered from a crime scene, whereas only one of those DNA fingerprints had been included in the report the police received. While the eyes of Kazinski became bigger and bigger behind his round spectacles, Braun changed his tone and warned him that it would be wise to cooperate, or else there would be serious consequences. His voice became even higher as Kazinski tried to deny and squeeze himself out of this precarious situation. At one stage he blamed 'this *Fraulein* Malzberger' for cheating. I nearly interrupted with "You'd better leave Monica Malzberger out of this!" but Braun was quicker and remarked that this was a matter between himself and Kazinski, without a need to get other people or members of his staff involved. I concentrated on my role as an expert and observer, and kept quiet.

Eventually, the Director realized he was cornered. With drooping shoulders he admitted he had not informed the Chief Inspector about all the DNA evidence that had been obtained.

"Now we're making progress," commented Braun with a hint of satisfaction. Kazinski asked for a withdrawal of the report he had handed in, so he could replace it with an accurate copy. He further promised that from now on all reported results would be flawless (I recalled he had still not handed over the results of the hair samples from the second case), all data would be trustworthy, and this would never happen again, etcetera, etcetera.

He was given a second chance with a new assignment. He would receive one or two swabs, and was asked to compare their DNA with filed records including those of the crime scene hair samples.

"So from now on I trust you report the true outcome of your experiments," Braun concluded. On a more positive note, he added, if Kazinski now fully cooperated the 'incident' would be downplayed and there might not even be long-term consequences. I couldn't help pursing my lips at that comment; surely the Head of the Forensic Institute had deserved some way of punishment after what he had done? But I was a mere observer and couldn't comment. At least I was certain that Kazinski would double-check that all future PCRs were performed and reported correctly, whether carried out by Gudrun or by any other technician.

***

It was Thursday night and I was preparing myself to go to the health/sex club again. Florian Helmuth had replied to my email that he agreed with my assessment. He had promised to hand over a DNA sample as soon as possible, maybe even tomorrow, together with a public statement (I gathered his lawyers were still brewing over this) after which he would be travelling for a few days. That meant that Kazinski could soon compare his and Bamberg's DNA fingerprint with those obtained from the crime scenes. I was impatient to learn the results of that experiment. Moreover, Helmuth had confirmed that I had been his invitee to *In Corpore Sano*. My membership had been accepted (and the monthly fee had already been cashed from my bank account) so I prepared my next visit. I had to wear the same outfit as last time, since I wasn't prepared to invest more money in that kind of 'sportswear'. Unfortunately, I had not reckoned with Robert. He entered the bedroom without a warning – he didn't know I was changing in there. When he saw me he looked surprised, then started laughing.

"What is that you're wearing? What on Earth are you planning tonight?" I didn't know how to talk myself out of this, so why not tell him the truth?

"I'm trying to look like a hooker. What do you think, do I pass the test?" and made a pirouette to display every side of my body. He shook his head in disbelief.

"Sue, what's going on here? You're joking, aren't you? You're not seriously going out like that?" I assured him there was no harm in it.

"It is for a girl's party, at a private house, so don't worry – men won't be permitted. I'll wear something over it before I leave the house." His response surprised me:

"You'd better not address any men in the street on your way. And when you come home, sweetie, I want to strip you out of those clothes with my own hands. No, wait, I think you owe me a striptease tonight. How about that?" Now it was my time to laugh. But he made sure I had my phone with me, and said I shouldn't hesitate to call the police immediately, should anything run out of hand. With that assurance, he let me go, reluctantly.

***

When I entered the health club, the young receptionist greeted me with a smile. This time I was alone in the changing room, but when I entered the fitness studio, the same two women were chatting on their exercise bikes as last time. One of them had platinum-blond hair, worn in the style of Greta Garbo. She had called her friend, whose hair was darker blonde with some reddish streaks in it, Lea. When they saw me they greeted me with a nod and continued their conversation.

I mounted my stepper and started my warming up, ignoring the men who were walking around and testing the flesh (one did so literally: he squeezed the ladies in their buttocks, which resulted in faked giggles. Fortunately, he didn't try that with me!). After a while, I decided to have a word with the two girls.

I walked up to their bikes (they were hardly moving the pedals) and introduced myself:

"Hi, I'm Sue. I remember you two were here last Tuesday." They giggled.

"We're always here, babe!" said Greta Garbo. The other introduced herself:

"Hi Sue, I'm Lea, and this is Tini. Welcome to the club! Is that

English accent genuine?"

I confessed being British. Then I explained that, still being new to the place, I would appreciate if the two could keep an eye on me.

"You don't have to feel afraid, babe, nobody is going to harm you. Carlo will be here the moment one of these pigs touches you without your permission." I followed Lea's view up, towards a CCTV that hung from the ceiling. Now I noticed the other cameras; there wasn't a corner of this room not covered by their view. Apparently these were connected to a screen that Carlo the barkeeper could see. If these two ladies put their trust in this security system, I'd have to do so, too. I nodded and relaxed my shoulders, thanked them and went off to continue my exercise on the stepper. Meanwhile, I considered these two ladies could actually be helpful, if they were indeed always present here. In addition, given they could spend their hours here at leisure, it would not be suspicious if I did the same.

In fact, the evening was rather relaxing, and I no longer felt ridiculous in my outfit. I got used to the glances, and paid little attention to the 'pigs' that swarmed around us women. I fitted in with the others, although it was certainly not my intention to meet the requirement of six dates per month. The CCTVs didn't leave my thoughts. Steffan Braun could ask for their records, I guessed, in case he could come up with serious reasons to suspect this health club being involved with the murders. But would that help? I considered it unlikely the records of the past four months, if they still existed, would show anything that could offer a clue. We were looking for something more subtle, something not so obvious. At least, that was what I was looking for.

Later that evening I went back to Tini and Lea for another chat. It seemed they had accepted me as one of them. Socializing was easy but superficial in this environment. Nobody would disclose personal information. I'd have to trust them, hoping they would trust me, without breaking the social codes of this place. Since our chatting developed nicely, I gave it a try:

"You know what, girls, I have a problem. In fact, I have two problems, but one is acute. Last Tuesday there was a man sitting in the bar who knows me from my previous life. You can imagine I don't want to be confronted with a scene, and neither would he, you get it? Can you keep him away from me? He was sitting in the corner. Beard, dark blond, small bald patch at the back of his head, tall posture. He was with a blonde girl in pink whose name I don't know. Short hair." It was all I could remember.

"That was probably Gina with her customer," said Tini. "Don't worry, he isn't in today. And it is easy to avoid him because he never is, Thursdays." That was good to know.

"And what's your other problem, babe? Not that I'm curious, but I'd like to know!" Lea appeared the more inquisitive of the two. A man approached us and mocked:

"Ladies, if you don't move those pretty legs they'll become all flabby and fat. And I prefer firm flesh, right?" he walked up to Tini and put a hand on her thigh, to demonstrate what he meant.

"Tight and firm, just what I like!" he commented, while he tried to move his hand towards her inner leg and up. The gesture failed, as Tini was still sitting on the bike and started spinning a bit faster, shoving his hand away with the movement. She smiled at him, with her unnaturally full, pink painted lips:

"I'll be in the bar in five minutes, sweetheart," and, when he lingered close to her:

"Off you go! Order me a cocktail! Carlo knows my preference." He obeyed immediately and left.

"Your other problem?" repeated Lea, as if nothing had happened.

"I hope I can trust the two of you…" They both made a swearing gesture while they exclaimed they were completely trustworthy. They bent over, hoping for a conspiracy that they could be part of, and I lowered my voice to a whisper to increase the sense of secrecy:

"I keep worrying about these two colleagues who died. You know, Lena and Laila. You both knew them, didn't you?" They backed off with faces of disgust, as if I had opened a stinking cheese, their heavily painted eyes wide open now.

"*Bist du 'ne Bulle oder was*? How do you know they were one of us?" Lea hissed under her voice. No, I wasn't a cop, I assured them, hand on my heart. Tini whispered:

"Are you investigating? Like a private detective?" That would do. It was a good excuse for my activities. My mentioning of the two killed women had changed their moods. They were both quiet for a moment. Then Tini softly said:

"Actually, Lena was a bitch. I didn't like her – though of course I didn't want her dead. But Laila was sweet. Wasn't she?" She turned to her friend for support.

"Oh yea, really sweet. She hadn't been here that long yet. I still think about her, sometimes…" This was an opening for me.

"You two could really help me with my investigations. I need to know who, of all the ladies belonging to this club, has an arrangement for the coming Sunday. If you could get that information," (in my thoughts I added *with the discretion that is typical for your profession*) "that would be great. But please, don't disclose to anybody who I am. Not even the girls must know our little secret. So ask your questions in a way nobody is suspicious, especially not Carlo. Can I count on you?" Oh yes, they liked it! Secrets are ever so attractive. It was probably the most exciting evening these two girls had had for a long time. They both nodded vigorously, with their silicone-filled lips closed tight to indicate they would be silent like a grave. I now had two assistants, who would also act as my guardian angels. Maybe they could extract the required information from him without raising suspicion. Steffan would be pleased.

Since Tini and Lea would be here tomorrow night as well, they could take over for me, and I could avoid being seen by Günther Müller. I gave the girls my cell phone number and instructed them to call me when they had found out anything of relevance. Then I went to the bar for a well-deserved drink, and openly flirted with a few men. I felt much more secure than I did two nights ago, with Carlo the barkeeper as my bodyguard. It had been a good evening. I relaxed and played my role with more enthusiasm than I had imagined I would be capable of. Soon, a middle-aged man seated himself next to me at the bar and started a conversation. He was good-looking, I had to admit, and he behaved well-mannered. He treated me with a degree of respect that I had not expected at all. I started to realize that this club indeed had something to offer to the 'girls': here they could meet customers of a kind that would be hard to find otherwise. My partner of the night introduced himself as Mark. First names sufficed here. Mark turned out to be an excellent conversationalist, keeping to a subject just long enough to reach a satisfying level of depth, and changing it just before it became boring. He asked for my opinion on a number of subjects, invited me to share my thoughts with him, and seemed genuinely interested in my views. In return I enjoyed listening to his voice, and soon I forgot my environment or the role I had to play tonight.

I returned back to reality when he put an arm around my shoulder. By now I had had enough to drink to be truly relaxed. I liked his touch. He smelled nice. Thoughts about emotions that are ruled by smells, with scientific theories about existing or non-existing human pheromones were pushed to the background by feelings of satisfaction, happiness and, I had to admit it, lust. I could spend a night with this man. Chances were I would enjoy it. More than the matrimonial sex that had become a bit stale over the years.

His hand had moved from caressing my shoulder to a more erotic part of my body. Carlo was watching us from a distance. I had noticed his red little book in which he wrote down the arrangements of the night. When he caught my eye he looked at me inquisitively. Would this be my first date for the club?

Finally I woke up from my dream. No way I was going that route! With regret in my voice (which I meant) I told Mark I wasn't ready for this yet. He didn't seem to mind, at least he didn't show disappointment. He said he had liked the company, to which I responded that I had really enjoyed the conversation. I ended it there. Carlo looked slightly discontented but I didn't care. Maybe some other night I would have the guts, but right now I wanted to be home.

When I finally returned to my real life and in my own house, I ignored my marital troubles for the moment and was able to show Robert a side he didn't know I had in me.

## XXI

On Friday, Kazinski reported the results of the DNA tests. He must have forced his technician to drop everything else to get the results in so quickly. Steffan called me late that afternoon. The results were as we had expected. One of the black hairs recovered from the body of Lena Lotus belonged to Reiner Bamberg: the DNA matched. The other two hairs produced no match to the database (it was the DNA fingerprint of one of those other hairs that Kazinski had used in his false report). The hair of Florian Helmuth matched one of the blond hairs recovered from dead Laila; the other blond hair drew a negative in the database. Furthermore, he had a confession from Bamberg that he had been a member of that club until the end of past December. With this data, Steffan was now also convinced that the killer had chosen both his murder victims and his press victims through *In Corpore Sano*.

"However, Bamberg wasn't being blackmailed, or so he says. So what was the point of those letters?" Steffan wondered. I had to think for a moment.

"Maybe the killer just wanted more press coverage of the murders. It worked, didn't it?"

"And hopefully we've put an end to that. I've sent out an official press release that clears both Bamberg and Helmuth, based on their DNA samples. And we stick to our original version that there is no relation between the two murders, at least, that is what we will tell the press." With that he ended the call.

It was ludicrous. First the press speculated on a connection between two murders while the police denied it, being misled by fabricated DNA evidence that put them on the wrong track. Now that they had the true results, with two matching DNA fingerprints, produced and reported by Kazinski's lab without manipulation, the police knew there was a connection but lied about it to the press. I wondered how Braun could get away with that. But if this calmed down the expanding impact of the murders, the killer would be upset. He would be forced to make a move. And it was our goal to stop him while he moved, but before he could kill again. There was not much time left. I counted on Lea and Tini now.

***

I needed to concentrate. Time was running out. The publisher had asked for a progress statement and I had hardly worked on my book these past few weeks. My predicted date for the next murder was only two days off. I was really getting nervous. Why didn't Lea or Tini call? Were there no dates arranged for this Sunday, or had they failed to extract the essential information from Carlo, or from the other female members of the health club? The minutes ticked away slowly. I considered calling them – and then I didn't. Please let there not be another murder! *Concentrate on your book, Sue, and let's wait for developments to come*. There was nothing else I could do. Once the girls confirmed which dates were arranged for Sunday I would contact Steffan, urging for police assistance to protect the prostitutes in question, but without knowing a particular time and address, there was very little I could do. I reread the text I had just written. It was all nonsense so I deleted it again. *Try to concentrate, Sue!*

Time passed. Nothing happened. This was so nerve-racking! I couldn't eat, my pulse was elevated, I kept checking my phone. Still nothing. The day passed and no news. I felt sick.

***

I was preparing dinner for one (as Robert was away for an editorial meeting in Oxford) when finally the telephone rang. But it wasn't from Lea or Tini: it was Monica.

"Hello Dr. Swanson, have you heard the news yet?" she asked eagerly. The knot inside my stomach pulled tight.

"What news?"

"I just heard it myself. Gudrun Wenzel is dead – you know, the technician from the Forensic Institute. She was found dead in her apartment this morning. I heard it from Katja, my friend and colleague who still works there. Apparently she has committed suicide. Isn't that terrible?"

I had to swallow. This couldn't be true. It was the wrong date, the wrong person, the wrong type of death. I couldn't take the news in and asked Monica to repeat what she had just said with all the details she knew. Thoughts tumbled in my head. Was Gudrun a member of *In Corpore Sano*? Was the victim really Gudrun? Was it really suicide? Had she been blackmailed? I tried to calm my breathing while I expressed my sympathy. Although Monica hadn't liked Gudrun, she still sympathised with her former colleague and competitor. I finished the call as best as I could and switched off the oven. I was no longer hungry. I had to sit down and could do with a drink right now.

Robert would be away all weekend. There was nobody to talk to, nobody to share the news with, to express my doubts, to listen to my questions. Should I call Steffan? Would he be in charge of a presumed suicide? Could I still expect something to happen the day after tomorrow, the fourth of April, the date I had calculated as the most probable for a next murder?

I collapsed on the couch with the half-emptied glass of whiskey on the table in front of me, exhausted and at my wits' end. I closed my eyes and tried to exclude the world for a moment.

When I opened them, I saw dots and checker boards that moved in and out of my vision, flickering, flashing, forming concentric circles that slowly increased in size.

Expanding circles.

The aura lasted for about twenty minutes. By the time the nausea worsened it was too late to take any medication. The headache hit me like a blow. I crawled to my room, unable to stand up, disgusted by every smell, sound or light that reached my oversensitive senses. The migraine attack lasted until Sunday night. It was the worst weekend I could remember. I wished I were dead.

***

The headache subdued Sunday evening. After a night of deep sleep I woke up on Monday morning with an unusually light feeling in my head but without headache, and with a ravaging hunger. After a long shower I ate an enormous breakfast to make up for a weekend without food, and then sent a text message to Steffan: '*I don't know how busy you are right now but pls. call me when you have the time. Best, Sue*'. I cleaned up the kitchen, changed my bed linens, and while the washing machine was humming I turned back to my computer in an attempt to make up for the lost time.

Steffan called around lunchtime.

"Hi Sue, what's up, how was your weekend?" he asked politely.

"Not very good, I'm afraid: I was defeated by a terrible migraine attack. Don't get those very often, but if one hits me, it's serious." He expressed his sympathy.

"But that's not why I asked you to call me. I guess you're busy now with the new case?"

"What case?"

"I mean the so-called suicide of this technician from the Forensic Institute. She died on Saturday. Surely you're investigating?" I couldn't imagine he wasn't.

"So far that case has not landed on my desk. My understanding is that the woman committed suicide, and the usual procedures are followed. Once Pathology has handed in their report we will have a definite, but so far the case is treated as suicide, which isn't my responsibility." As an afterthought he added: "I don't see how this is related to the murder cases, in case that's what you're thinking?"

"Oh come on, Steffan! The victim is the technician who produced the falsified PCR reactions that Kazinski originally reported. We confronted him with our knowledge only a few days ago. Now she's dead. You can't seriously think there is no connection? I mean, can you be certain she killed herself? She may have been forced to do so, she may have been blackmailed, or it may have been murder, disguised as suicide. Maybe someone wanted to silence here. And there's more: she is the..." But Steffan interrupted me:

"Hang on, Sue, don't get carried away, please. Right now we have no reason to believe there is a connection. We will wait for the pathological report, and if there is anything suspicious it will be picked up. Trust me, our people are doing their jobs, and they do them thoroughly. Now, as for your predicted murder date, I'm sorry to disappoint you, but so far we have had no report of a prostitute being murdered yesterday..." I couldn't be certain, but there seemed to be a touch of irony in his voice.

I knew. My prediction had been false. Nevertheless, something had happened this weekend, and it had to do with the case, I was certain about the connection. But I needed to be patient. I asked Steffan to share the outcome of the pathological report with me, once it became available. He replied that he would see what he could do. On a more positive note, he added, they had now started an official investigation of *In Corpore Sano*, their owners and the administration of that club. They would soon start analysing the CCTV recordings and the bookkeeping of the arranged sex meetings. The fact that both murder victims and both press leaks were linked to this health club were sufficient to extend the investigations into that direction. He added that the owners had been cooperative so far.

I sighed. It wouldn't result in anything, I feared. I was convinced the meetings that had produced the killings had not been included in Carlo's books. The CCTV recordings might cover a few days or weeks at the most, but it was highly unlikely that they would disclose anything to do with the murders.

"I can't say I fancy the idea of you browsing through the records of the past two weeks; you'll have a chance to view me in rather, what shall I say, unusual clothing. But there is little I can do to prevent that, is there?"

"Don't worry, I have seen worse things in my life," was his dry reply. That didn't sound like a compliment, did it?

With that, the call ended. I was a bit disappointed in him. Instead of investigating the death of Gudrun, they zoomed in on the health club. Although I still believed the club could hide valuable clues, I doubted if the books or the CCTV recordings would reveal them. He didn't welcome any advise from me any more, but could I blame him? I had put him on the wrong track, got him in trouble more than once, and nothing I had done so far had brought him any closer to solving two murder cases. I was a lousy crime investigator.

***

When Robert came home that night, I made an effort to hide my bad mood, realizing he would probably see through my attempts. He suggested we dine out, as we often did when he returned from his travels, so that we could catch up with each other. The choice of restaurant was easy: without considering alternatives, he drove us straight to Giovanni's *Albergo*. We were greeted with a big smile.

"*Signora Sue, Signore Roberto, Buone sera! Le due?*" asked the owner as we both came in together, thanks to a parking space just in front of the restaurant. He pronounced my name as 'Soo-eh', in lack of an Italian form of my name. We confirmed it was only the two of us tonight.

Robert decided on the wine, while I inspected the menu. I chose the day's special, which made my husband have the same. No longer able to pretend, I said:

"It was a hard day for me, dear, don't be cross that I'm not in such a good mood." He asked for the reason – he always did when I confessed things weren't going right. I decided to tell him about my investigations. I told him about the faulty DNA results reported to the police, that Steffan Braun was leading the investigations (he remembered him vaguely, school affairs had been mostly my responsibility), and about the latest developments, the presumed suicide, my suspicion that this had to be linked to the previous murders, the denial by the police, my wrong prediction... the words flew as if a sluice had opened. The only part I left out was the role of the sex club and my attendance there. My husband listened quietly and attentively. He recognized my need to share this with him.

By the time I was finished, our *antipasti* had arrived.

We ate in silence for a few minutes. Finally, Robert put his fork down and commented:

"From what you told me, I can't really see a connection yet. You described the previous murders as 'expanding circles', but how would this suicide expand the circles even more, if it were murder instead? Was this technician famous?"

It was a logical question that I had asked myself as well.

"She wasn't special as far as I know. I don't see how her death can expand the circles. It seems to draw a new circle instead, maybe intercepting with the others. I don't see how, but my gut feeling tells me this interception is the clue to the solution. I wish I knew how to interpret it all."

"My dear, your gut feeling has been more often right than wrong. I would suggest you put it aside for a while. It is no use forcing yourself thinking about it. Your Eureka moment will come, but you'll have to allow your unconscious brain to work on it. Which it can't as long as you're actively thinking about it."

Robert was trying to help me, comfort me and at the same time assure me. Just like he had always done. Why did he make an effort to be a good husband – was he making up for his bad behaviour? I couldn't help thinking there was another Robert who had entered our marriage, one I couldn't trust, one who betrayed me. I tried my best not to spoil the evening.

"You are right. Let's change the subject. How was your trip?" He told about his travels, multiple meetings with colleagues, bureaucratic hurdles, complications with travel visas, and more. I listened absentmindedly, nodding and confirming at the right intervals. It helps to be married for over twenty-five years to keep a conversation going without paying too much attention.

By the time dessert was served, Robert changed the subject on his own.

"Sue, your birthday is coming up soon. You haven't mentioned anything you're planning, so may I make a suggestion?" That was new! Robert wasn't the type to remember birthdays or anniversaries. My birthday was in five days from now and I had not made any plans yet.

"Go on, I'm all ears!" I was really eager to hear his thoughts.

"Why don't you keep the date free, and I'll take you out. How's that?"

I said I'd like that, very much so, what a nice idea, etcetera, the sort of things one says on such an occasion. But in the back of my mind the nagging feeling of jealousy grew by the minute. Why this sudden attention? It wasn't like Robert at all to ask me out, these days. Whenever we went out, a concert, a visit to a museum, meeting up with friends, it had most often been my initiative. He hardly ever invited me out. Surely he was compensating for his behaviour. Jealousy is a disease, like a malicious growth that increases in size over time. I had to fight back my feelings.

"I'm looking forward to the surprise, as long as you tell me what I'm supposed to wear for the occasion," I joked. Not wanting to spoil the evening, I concentrated on the *tartuffa* in front of me and blocked any negative thoughts. The wine did the rest, and soon blocked any serious thoughts at all.

# XXII

The message Monica had left on my landline was short: “We need to talk urgently.” She had sounded agitated, not at all herself. She had not explained what was so urgent, and I couldn’t think of a reason. I had called her back the next morning and we arranged to meet at the lunchroom that had become our regular meeting place. Now I waited impatiently to hear what was so urgent.

To my surprise she didn’t come alone. She brought another young woman who I didn’t know, a slender, frail-looking girl wearing skinny jeans that made her thin legs appear even thinner.

“Dr. Swanson, this is my friend Katja. She is a technician at the Forensic Institute, we have been working together. Katja called me last night because she had a problem at work, and the only person I could think of to help her is you. Would you mind listening to her story?”

Katja looked insecure and embarrassed, and sat down with a feeble smile, trying to be invisible. I gave her an encouraging look and proposed we have a drink while we chatted, but Katja refused to order anything. To be coherent with her friend, Monica refused anything for herself as well, so I had to enjoy my fruit juice all by myself.

“So Katja, tell me your story,” I invited her after I had tried my best to put her at ease.

She was obviously uncomfortable with the situation, but as she started talking the words came more fluently with every sentence. Recently she had been given a swab sample to do a PCR fingerprint on. The sample had come from a crime scene (what else) and had produced a high DNA yield, which made it really easy to get confidential results. Her negative control had been negative, the positive control positive, basically, everything had been just like it is written in the textbooks. Until she checked the obtained fingerprint in the database.

“I couldn’t believe the result. When I first saw the hit it came up with I got hot and cold at the same time." There was a quiver in her voice as she recalled the experience and her soft voice was now all but a whisper. "I thought there was a mistake, so I repeated the whole procedure, but the result was the same. Dr. Swanson, I can assure you, I have done this work for five years now, and I have never been in a position to question my own data. I have never had a contamination in my reactions…" She started to apologize for her results now, but she hadn't told me yet what was so surprising about them. I kindly interrupted:

"I have no doubt at all that you are a reliable technician. Just tell me what hit you found?"

She didn't give me the straight answer yet.

"As you know, the DNA fingerprints of all our colleagues are stored in our database, so that a contamination can be recognized when it occurs." I knew this. It was standard procedure to have the fingerprints of all lab workers included in the database. It enabled recognition of a contaminated sample, as in such a case the obtained fingerprint would be mixed with that of a lab worker, and the computer would be able to recognize this as such. I nodded to acknowledge I was aware of this.

"So when I found a hit, to my surprise it was a hit to a fingerprint marked 'II', for 'Internal Individual'. But the thing is, it couldn't be a contamination, because my negative control was negative. I only got that banding pattern in the real sample…"

"But Katja, a contamination can happen at any step: during sample preparation or DNA isolation, for example. It doesn't have to be during the PCR reaction, because, as you know, basically at every step of the procedure a contamination can happen. Had you performed the DNA isolation yourself? Is it possible the sample got contaminated during that procedure? Did you produce your own fingerprint? Or was it a colleague who had contaminated it? In any case, it's not a big deal. It is annoying, but not something to be ashamed of. Mistakes happen, you know!" I really couldn't see what the problem was.

"No, no, that isn't what happened, Dr. Swanson. See, I am not so much worried about an II result, it is the person whose fingerprint I got that gives me the shivers!" There was panic in her eyes as she said this.

"So who was it?" Now I was curious. Why was she so upset about it? She barely whispered the name.

"It is my boss, Dr. Kazinski!"

***

I had made a scheme on paper this time, reluctant to use a computer for anything related to my criminal investigations anymore. I had written down the names of all people involved so far, starting with the two victims, Lena and Laila, with the dates of their deaths behind their names. These, together with the names of Bamberg and Helmuth were included in a square labelled *In Corpore Sano*. Thin lines connected Lena to Bamberg and Laila to Helmuth. In order to represent all other members of that club, Lea and Tini were added in smaller writing, together with Carlo the barkeeper. These were the people I knew in the sex club, but clearly their small-printed names had nothing to do with the murders. The two journalists, Schramm and Dornfeld, were placed outside the square, as I had no reason to believe they were related to the club, but arrows linked Schramm with Helmuth and Dornfeld with Bamberg, each marked with the word 'letter'. The two letters both showed a line leading to a big question mark, as I still didn't know who the anonymous author had been. I was no longer certain this question mark also represented the murderer, so I didn't connect it to the two dead women.

On the other side of the square representing the sex club I had written down Kazinski's name, with an arrow to Gudrun, who unfortunately now also had a date behind her name. I forced myself to also add Katja, the technician who had obtained Kazinski's DNA fingerprint from a crime scene swab (represented as a dotted line). Then, with a sigh, I put Monica down, with a dotted line leading to Lena to represent she had produced the DNA results from that case.

I looked at my drawing and shook my head. It made no sense at all. There was nothing I could imagine that connected the left part of my scheme with the right part. No connection between Gudrun and the two prostitutes, other than the fact that she had worked for Kazinski and that Kazinski had initially faked his report on Lena's case; but Monica had also worked for Kazinski, and Katja was still part of his team. I drew a stronger line between Kazinski and Gudrun, marking it with a little heart, to indicate the two had been lovers. Was that relevant? Katja's name remained disconnected, because I didn't know where the swab sample had originated from that she had analysed.

Was the name of the murderer already included on this piece of paper, or should I add 'M.' for him? Was the murderer of Lena and

Laila also responsible for the death of Gudrun, or had she really killed herself? Questions, questions! Should I add the theft of my computer to this scheme, too? It would be connected to Schramm, and I could add an 'X' for the young thief who had committed the crime on his command, not knowing his name, but that wouldn't help. I couldn't make sense of this. I crumpled the piece of paper up and threw it with so much force in the paper basket that it tumbled. *Don't waste your time, Sue, you have better things to do!* With a sigh, I forced my concentration back to my book.

I was startled by the sound of a key being inserted in the lock of our front door. Was it that late already? Robert peeked his head through my door to say hello. When he saw I wasn't actually typing he came in and seated himself in the reading chair in front of my bookcase.

"How was your day?" he asked in a casual manner. It wasn't like him to be so attentive. I told him I had seen Monica in the morning but I wasn't in the mood to elaborate on our meeting, or to tell about her troubled colleague. I wasn't in the mood for small talk at all. He didn't seem to notice.

"So… about Saturday," he abruptly changed the subject. Oh dear, my birthday was only two days away! I had completely forgotten about it.

"We will go out, as I had said, and I suggest you wear that blue dress. You know which one I mean, I like to see you in it. And wear comfortable shoes, please. Comfortable and elegant. After all, you can still show your legs!" With a little giggle he stood up and left me in utter bewilderment, commenting on his way out that he had brought some French cheese, in case I wanted some.

What was wrong with my spouse? He suddenly behaved like the ideal husband, he wanted me to look smart, told me which dress to wear… then I recalled I had actually asked him for a dressing code myself. And then that comment about shoes! Female shoes are *either* elegant *or* comfortable. It can't be both. What was he planning? Comfortable shoes would do for walking, a visit to a museum or a city tour maybe, but why the dress? Why did I have to be elegant? Were we going to meet a VIP he needed to impress? I had no idea what to expect and, for a change, I wasn't looking forward to being surprised on my birthday. I feared my husband no longer had nice surprises up his sleeve.

***

The announcement of the funeral caught my eye by accident. I don't normally read the local obituaries and funeral notices, but when I was folding out a discarded newspaper to protect my kitchen table for repotting a plant, I noticed the name: Gudrun Wenzel. The date of the funeral happened to be today, in three hours from now. After giving it some thought, I called Monica to ask if she had seen the announcement. She knew about it, and would attend to support Katja, who felt obliged to go to the funeral of her colleague. I spontaneously offered to join them. Not that I am fond of funerals, but I wanted to know if Kazinski would be there, and how he would react. I was reluctant to ask Monica to spy on him.

The celebration was held in a small church in one of the villages that had been swallowed by the city. It was a serene event. Gudrun didn't seem to have an extended family: I could only identify her mother, who was heartbroken with the loss of her daughter. She was comforted by two elderly ladies, sisters of her maybe, or friends. Many villagers were there, men and women of approximately Gudrun's age condoled the mother, and together with the members of the local choir, in which Gudrun had sung, more than half the church was filled. The conductor of the choir held a short speech, after which they sang a Bach choral, accompanied by the church organ. It was a moving gesture. Amongst the people present I recognized quite a few laboratory colleagues, and Katja pointed out members of the younger generation that I had never met. Dr. Kazinski was there, too. He didn't speak in public. He had come unaccompanied and had seated himself apart from his colleagues. He appeared to be heartbroken and had to fight back his tears. Either he was a good actor, or he had really been fond of the deceased. It seemed he, together with the mother, were the most grieved by the loss of Gudrun of all those present in the church.

***

Eventually I called Lea myself, because I had decided to cease my criminal investigations. She gave me lots of excuses why she hadn't called: she had been busy, and it wasn't so easy to talk to the other girls, some of whom were jealous of her, Carlo never left the book out of his sight, and Tini hadn't really helped, etcetera. It no longer mattered. I told her there had been a false alarm, and nothing had happened that weekend, so everything was fine. I apologized in case she had been worried. She asked if we would see each other on Thursday? I kept my answer vague, but wasn't really planning to go to the club anymore. My prediction about a third murder had been wrong, and I wasn't sure about any of my hypotheses any more. I was completely fed up with the whole affair and wished I had never gotten involved.

I wanted to put all this to an end and continue being a scientist and author – at least I was not a complete failure in my own profession! But there was one more thing to do: I had promised Katja to help her, and that meant another visit to the police station. It wouldn't be an easy visit.

# XXIII

Steffan Braun was obviously irritated. He had not been keen on this meeting and he had tried to avoid it. I insisted that I needed to talk to him as soon as possible. Obviously, he didn't appreciate that I was interfering with his work once more. I couldn't blame him. But it had to be.

There had been one detail in Katja's story that didn't fit and that I couldn't explain. She had not obtained a mixture of two fingerprints, which is what you expect when a sample gets contaminated. Instead, she had only gotten one DNA fingerprint, that of Kazinski, from a sample that had produced a high DNA yield. I had specifically asked her about a background signal due to a second individual, but there hadn't been any. That was odd. It seemed as if the sample had contained DNA from the Director of the Institute right from the beginning. I needed to know where that sample came from, but Katja didn't know. Steffan could tell me, but, as he made it quite obvious, he wasn't very cooperative this time.

We were seated in his office, he behind his desk and myself in front of it, just like the first time we discussed forensic results. And like the first time, he behaved formally, distanced, and protective.

I ignored his attitude and told him that I had confidential information about a test performed at the Forensic Institute.

"You didn't break in again, did you?" He asked it with more disapproval in his voice than was needed.

"No, the test was performed by a technician as part of her daily procedures, and she contacted me about it in private. She is in a difficult position due to the results she obtained. The outcome was very surprising, and we can't make sense of it. For reasons that I can't explain to you right now, the technician is reluctant to report her results to her supervisor, as she fears the consequences. She came to me for help, and I think you might be able to solve our little mystery." Braun just frowned, and commented that I was talking riddles. I knew it was hard to understand what this was about, since I couldn't tell the complete story, at least not yet.

"Steffan, the only thing I'd like to know from you is this: did you send a sample to the Institute in the past few days that could, in any way, be connected to the two murder cases? Or to the suicide of Gudrun Wenzel?" I didn't say 'presumed suicide' this time. I didn't want to upset him more than he already was.

"It isn't really any of your business, is it? But as a matter of fact, we have sent a sample from the suicide case for further investigation. The autopsy had shown that she had had… well, in any case, we sent a swab for an ID to the Forensic Institute."

He kept the details back, but the fact that he was willing to talk to me about it made me a bit more cooperative, too.

"It seems that sample came back with a hit in the database. Apparently, it contained the DNA of Dr. Kazinski himself," I informed him in a neutral voice.

"What??" Braun now sat upright in his chair, looking bewildered.

"So you understand why the technician couldn't report the results to her boss: she would have had to tell him it was his own DNA that had been recovered from a crime scene. Do you mind if I ask what the origin of your swab sample was?" I asked it as politely as I could. But he no longer listened, occupied with his own thoughts.

"Who would have thought... It means we have a suspect, and not just anybody…" Braun was talking more to himself than to me, but his remark made me sit upright this time.

"A suspect? So there was something suspicious about the death of Gudrun after all?"

He sighed. And then he talked. It turned out the autopsy of the poor woman had not only confirmed her death by strangulation, due to the rope around her neck from which she had been found hanging. They had also found fresh bruises on her wrists and ankles. These could be taken as evidence of violence: a fight, harsh treatment, or even a form of torture. It had been enough reason to take a swab sample. With my piece of information on the identity of that DNA, Steffan was now speculating that Gudrun may have died in a violent situation, and that Kazinski was a prime suspect. I concluded from this all that the case might be related to the two murdered prostitutes after all, but considered it wiser to keep my speculation to myself.

"So there were signs of violence on her body. Kazinski obviously didn't leave a hair at the crime scene, he couldn't, could he, given he is bald. You had sent a swab sample to his lab, but what was it taken from? The bruises on her wrists or on her ankles?"

"Neither. There is something else I haven't told you yet. The victim had had sexual intercourse not long before she died. The swab was a semen sample. So we're dealing with a sexual crime here, obviously... Kazinski.... who would have thought..."

Oh no! A wrong track again! I couldn't believe it!

"Steffan, they were lovers!" I cried out. His eyes widened. "Gudrun Wenzel and Gottfried Kazinski were lovers! I have seen them cuddling up in the... it doesn't matter. Believe me, they were lovers, so it is no surprise that you found his DNA inside her. It may not be related to her cause of death at all!"

It took him a second to digest this information. The bruises may have been the result of a sex game. There had been no other evidence of violence. Kazinski may have been the last person to see her alive and he may have even tied her down to toy with her, but I considered it highly unlikely he had killed her.

So what had happened after their last rendezvous? Had he told her he wanted to end the relationship, and had she taken that so badly that she hung herself? So shortly after having a hot bondage session? That was highly unlikely. I remembered how emotional Kazinski had been at the funeral. He had been in love with the woman and his grief had seemed genuine. Or was he tortured by feelings of guilt? I asked Steffan what he planned next.

"It would be best to confront Kazinski with the facts, and to let him tell his part of the story." He had regained his calmness again. I asked if he could break the news in such a way that the technician wouldn't have to fear any consequences. He suggested arranging a meeting at the Institute, so that the girl could disclose her findings to her boss in the presence of the Chief Inspector. That would protect her from any panicking response from her boss, and stop Kazinski from falsifying unwelcome results again. After that, he would ask Katja to leave, so that Kazinski could talk freely. How smart! It was the best option to get the truth out of Kazinski and still give him a chance to preserve his dignity in front of his personnel. He could make up a story to explain to Katja how she obtained his fingerprint later, and save his reputation. But Steffan made it clear I would not be invited to the meeting. It didn't matter. Now that Katja would not be in trouble as a result of her findings, I had done everything that was on my list before I could put this to rest. I was going to stop my investigations here and now!

Wishing each other a nice weekend, we parted in better spirits than we had started this meeting. I had finished my to-do list. My unofficial careers as criminal investigator, private detective or personal coach were over. It was time to turn the page and continue with my real life.

***

The sound of cutlery in the kitchen woke me up. The bedside next to me was empty. I groaned. He wasn't preparing breakfast in bed, was he? I hated breadcrumbs in bed, and drinking hot coffee while half lying down wasn't very comfortable, either. But I wouldn't spoil the day. Robert came in carrying a tray on which he had mounted toast, glasses with orange juice, cups for coffee and all the pots of marmalade and jam he had been able to find in my cupboards.

"I'll fetch the coffee and the cheese, love, they didn't fit on my tray." He was gone again before I could say anything. When he returned he finally wished me happy birthday with a kiss and a hug.

We had breakfast together and eventually I asked him how my day would be. Supposedly I was free to do whatever I wanted, as long as I was back home and ready by 6 p.m. for him to 'take me out'. I tried to convince him it would be better to tell me what he was up to, but he kept silent about his little secret.

When the telephone rang he sprung up to answer the call. He came back with the telephone in his hand, mouthing it was Jonathan. My eldest son was an early riser, and since he knew I wouldn't be sleeping in, he had called early to wish me a happy birthday. We chatted some, but when he asked what my plans for today were I had to pass the telephone back to his father, who disappeared out of earshot before answering.

A minute later he stuck his head around the bedroom door, still holding the phone, asking:

"Do you want Jonathan to come by today?" Why not, if I could spend most of the day as I pleased? It would be nice to have lunch together in honour of my birthday. I held out my hand to take over the phone again and made the arrangements with our son.

Later that morning I called Andrew, our youngest, who usually sleeps longer than his brother, to ask if he wanted to join us. They both lived in different cities where they were studying and each would need at least an hour by train to get here, so I had to make the call early enough for Andrew to be able to join our lunch (probably too early: his voice still sounded sleepy and I guess I had woken him up); nevertheless, he always welcomes a free lunch, so he agreed to be home at twelve thirty.

I considered where to take them. Their daily rations nowadays were refectory food alternated with junk food, so I wanted to offer them something decent for a change. After some thought I called the restaurant of the Zoo, which is famous for its lunches. I was lucky enough to get a table for three (Robert didn't want to join us, as he said he would keep his appetite for the evening) despite it being a Saturday.

The lunch with the boys turned out to be a success. I had often taken them to the Zoo when they were little, though we had rarely eaten at the restaurant, which was rather posh and not very child-friendly. Now they indulged in the lunch buffet and impressed me with the enormous amounts of food they could stow away. Memories of the past fed our conversation. I tried to get information from Jonathan about what his father had in store for me, but I didn't succeed.

"He wouldn't tell, all he said was that it was a matter between you and him," he said, after he had emptied a mouthful of chicken breast with white wine sauce. Of course Robert would not have told him; he knew Jonathan couldn't keep a secret.

"What is the matter between mum and dad?" asked Andrew. So he didn't know either. It was useless.

After dessert, they suggested we visit the Zoo, like the old days, to see if everything was still as they remembered it. It was a hilarious experience. The cages were much smaller than they remembered, and a few displays had been changed to the more animal-friendly way that Zoos opt for nowadays, but the paths were still the same, and more and more memories returned as we wandered around. It was a wonderful afternoon, which distracted me from the surprise that was still ahead of me.

# XXIV

I will never forget the drive with Robert on that evening of my birthday. Whenever I think back to that night I feel my cheeks redden, and not because it was so pleasant.

I was wearing my blue dress and had done my hair the way he likes it. I had put on nail polish and was thoroughly groomed for an event whose nature I couldn't anticipate. I had chosen elegant shoes that squeezed my toes but otherwise were endurable for an evening. As soon as the car had left our street Robert started talking, his eyes on the road, his hands clutching the steering wheel, in a manner that suggested he had memorized a speech. I watched him in profile, noticing how grey his hair had turned lately, and how the years started to show in his face. We were both getting older. He kept on talking, not watching me once to check my reaction. He concentrated on his speech. I kept silent, but his words set one alarm bell off after another in my head. My thoughts raced in various directions.

He started by telling me how much he was aware of his shortcomings as a husband. He wasn't perfect, (*nobody is*, I though, *I have my flaws, too!* but I didn't interrupt him) and he knew he spent too much time on his work, and not enough time with me, and that he travelled far too much (*what changed? it had always been like that*). We were both living our own lives, sharing ever fewer experiences together (*but that didn't give you a reason to commit adultery,* I sneered inwardly), he had noted things got worse after the boys had left home, and if we continued this way it would be hard to stay together and grow old in harmony. (*How pathetic! What are you heading for, are you going to leave me now? Is this going to be a farewell party, are you going to propose a separation?*) Something had to change (*and a new woman in your life had made that change, right?*) ... He went on and on while his words cut through my heart like knives. The jealousy was back at full force. I clenched my fists in my lap, tightened my jaws, promising myself not to make a scene. *Not now, not on my birthday*!

I had paid no attention to where he was taking me. When the car decelerated I looked up through a mist of tears, only to see a half-filled car park that I didn't recognize.

"And therefore, my love, a few months ago I decided to change something," he said, in a cheerful manner that I considered completely inappropriate for the occasion. "I thought I needed a hobby, something to relax and enjoy. That's why I have been in town many a evening since, although I noticed you were getting worried." He now smiled to me. "It wasn't what you though, love, I did it all for you."

With that, he stopped the engine, got out of the car and gallantly opened the door at my side. With a small bow he said:

"Welcome to Saturday Night's Over-Fifties Dinner-and-Dance Party. Happy birthday!"

I remained seated, locked in my chair, looking bewildered at the enlightened entrance of a land house that I had never seen before. Dinner and dance? Robert couldn't even dance!

I took a deep breath and with weak knees I slowly got out of the car. Robert grabbed my elbow as I started swaying and finally noticed my perplexed look.

"What's wrong? Oh, sorry, don't take it personally: it had to be an 'over fifties' party, because all other dance parties organized in the area are disco-like events that I know you don't like. Don't pay attention to the oldies, we'll have fun, I promise. Because, you see, I have been taken dancing classes! My teacher told me I have made enough progress not to make a fool of myself. But it is up to you to judge. I'm still not a good leader, but you can teach me the finesses of that. Let's go in!"

The tension finally broke and my tears flew freely. An idiot! I had been a complete idiot! Those evenings he spent in town, the inexplicable phone calls, the female perfume on his cloths, there had been no affair after all! I put my face in his jacket in a vain attempt to hide my tears but couldn't control the sobs.

We spent at least half an hour on that car park talking, finally exchanging all those things we should have said to each other long ago. How worried, hurt and jealous I had been, which he had hardly noticed because I wouldn't express those feelings. How involved he got in his new hobby without realizing his secrecy was misunderstood. Intentions ... misinterpretations... I thought that you thought that … but that wasn't what I meant … how could I know … Sometimes it isn't easy to be married. Or, I should rather say, to keep a marriage going. Both parties need to communicate clearly, must pay attention to what the other says, means and does. That had obviously gone wrong with us.

Eventually I was calm enough to go in; I dashed for the Ladies' to redo my makeup. After that, we had an awful lot to discuss, over a very nice five-course dinner with superb wines and pleasant music. And Robert showed me his latest acquired skill: he wasn't as bad a dancer as I had always believed. We could, with a bit more practice, actually make quite a nice pair on the dance floor.

I didn't once feel my toes.

***

I felt much better than I had done for a long time. My marriage had been saved from a nonexistent intruder and without the worries about crimes that had been, or had unexpectedly not been committed, my stress factor was lowered by several units. Two new customers had contacted me, one of whom had already agreed on a collaboration. It was only a small assignment, but the small project had potential to develop into something bigger, eventually. Apart from that, I was able to concentrate on my writing again, and spent my spare time in the garden, which needed a lot of attention in spring, or on my bike, enjoying long rides in the beautiful German countryside while Nature exploded with its yearly astonishing display. We had agreed to attend a Dinner-and-Dance Saturday night at least once a month, 'so you can keep practicing' I had joked, but the truth was that we had both rather enjoyed it. The place where these parties were organized was a late nineteenth-century mansion that was now being exploited for weddings and parties. The idea of an over-fifties dinner-and-dance evening had arisen from the observation that senior guests were less comfortable with the two-tact rhythmic monotony of pop music that allowed foot-hopping only. Ballroom dancing had once been very popular in Germany, and many 'older' pairs still enjoyed it. The idea of a dinner-and-dance, once popular in the early seventies, was reinvented, for which the place was absolutely perfect: a beautifully decorated room with a large dance floor, around which dinner tables were placed. During these evenings all tables were laid for two, and the guests could enjoy a set menu that lasted till eleven, as each course was intermitted with half an hour of dancing. With their outstanding cuisine, they offered just the right mix of entertainment. The price of the tickets was at the higher end of the spectrum, which selected for a public similar to those visiting classical concerts. The age of the guests varied from around fifty to well over seventy, but it didn't matter. All those attending had a common interest in good food and managed a variety in dancing styles. The music (not live, as that would increase the price even more, but chosen with taste) served all preferences, from foxtrot and waltzes (clearly favoured by the elder couples) to rumba, samba and jive, which got the youngsters off their chairs. I had bought a few new outfits that I could move comfortably in, though the matter of the shoes remained unsolved, for the time being.

It was on our way to our second D-and-D evenings, as we had started to call it, when some unexpected roadworks forced us to take a different route through town. Behind the red-and-white striped bars that blocked our usual way the street had been flooded, which we interpreted to mean a water pipe had burst. Yellow shields with *'Umleitung'* led us to an alternative route. Since we weren't in a hurry, it didn't matter. Robert steered us through town while he was talking about his latest research project. I noticed we passed the main building of our bank, where not so long ago I had paid a visit anticipating a separation. How things had changed for the better, in such a short time!

Enjoying the delicate light of dusk, I viewed the streets, only half listening to the talking of my husband.

"I don't know why they are directing us this way, there must be shorter alternatives." He interrupted his own talking as he turned right, obeying the sign. We passed a woman who was walking in the same direction as we were driving. She wore a long trench coat with a tight belt to accentuate her narrow waistline; beautiful legs in high heels showed under the coat. Her strides were remarkably elegant, considering the height of her heels, and she walked if she were a model. Long chestnut hair waved gracefully around her shoulders with every step. Here movements had something feline. I recognized the smoothness, the suppleness… this had to be Janine, the young woman I had trained with in our gym. I raised a hand to greet her but she wasn't paying attention to the car that was passing her. Robert saw my gesture.

"You know her?" he asked, while he glanced in his mirror. I explained who it was.

"We have lost touch since she moved. I wonder if she is now living in this neighbourhood? I still have her telephone number somewhere… maybe I'll give her a ring some day."

"Why not?" he answered absentmindedly, not particularly interested in a vague acquaintance of mine. He continued his story about the research project, while my thoughts went back to Janine. If she lived in this part of town, would she have found a gym around here? I only knew one, and in that place her body and the way she moved it would produce more than just glances. *Stop thinking about it, Sue, you are no longer involved in that!* I tried to concentrate on Robert's story and uh-huh at the right moments.

***

A few days later I dug out the piece of paper on which Janine had scribbled her telephone number. I don't know why I did that, I had deserted closer friends over the years, and I really didn't know her that well. But somehow this woman fascinated me, and I was curious to know how she was doing.

She answered my call immediately. I apologized in case I disturbed her, I just called for a little chat. It took her a moment to realize who I was, but then she was very friendly, and yes, of course, she had time, no problem.

"So have you settled in? All boxes unpacked?"

"Nearly! A couple of boxes are still in my study, but for the most part, I'm settled. I quite like it here," she replied. That's typical for a move; there always remain a few boxes unpacked. Wait for a year, and if they remain in that condition their contents are not important and one can do without them. I would dispose of their contents, but then, I am not a collector of things. But I know not all people are like that. Janine hadn't said where 'here' actually was.

"Could it be you moved to the eastern part of the centre? I think I saw you last Saturday night on the *Augustinerstraße*, you were afoot, in a trench coat, was that you?"

"Let me see, last Saturday… yes that is possible, I live not far from that street, do you know that area at all?" I didn't, and didn't visit that part of town very often.

"Not really, all I know is how hard it is to find a parking place around there," I joked. Janine had dealt with that problem by getting rid of her car, she told me.

"Well, that will help you keep in shape! Did you already find a gym close to where you live? I'm afraid I can't give you any advise on that, I have only heard about one place, and you'd better avoid that! It is called *'In Corpore Sano'* but from what I've heard about it it isn't a healthy place at all!" Why did I say this? What business was it to her that I knew the place, and why did I warn her to stay away from it? We had trained together, so a fitness studio was a suitable subject of conversation, but why mention this club? Too late now, I had said it. Instead of telling me it was up to her to choose a gym, her response was rather strange.

"How do you... I mean, well, no, I don't know the place. I haven't really had the time to look for a gym, will do so soon, I promise!" She tried to hide her confusion, but I could tell that name had not been new to her. Well, well. Before I could respond she said:

"Sorry, Sue, the doorbell rings. I have to hang up. It was lovely talking to you, take care! Bye!" and with that, she killed the line. I hadn't heard a doorbell, and she had ended the call unreasonably fast. Could it be I had mentioned something that she had no desire to talk about?

Or, and that was more likely, she considered me an intruder who should mind her own business and she was too polite to tell me so. *Sue, you're a moron!* It was too late now to apologize. No wonder I didn't have many friends, if I behaved like that. With a sigh, I went to the kitchen to empty the dishwasher and threw the piece of paper with her telephone number away.

# XXV

When I finally got my computer back it was a relief. The letter I received was an official invitation from the police that I could collect 'recovered goods' at such-and-such a time at the *Presidium*, by presenting this letter and a valid ID. My laptop was handed over to me by a fat lady in police uniform. The computer looked strangely familiar inside a sealed plastic bag with a label stuck onto it, which she scanned with a device just like those used at the supermarket. I had nearly taken my purse out of my pocket to pay – automated gestures can be powerful.

After three signatures I could finally take my computer home. I verified it wasn't damaged from the outside, though I couldn't check the hard disk as it wouldn't start up, due to an empty battery. Back home, after fifteen minutes of charging, it was revitalized and everything seemed to be OK. I spent a while updating my files, and then with a feeling of satisfaction I took my old desktop computer back to the attic.

Finally, life was back to normal. I informed the insurance company that I had gotten my computer back, and they could close the file. There was no need to claim any expenses.

I hadn't been in touch with Steffan Braun for quite a while now. I would have liked to know what had happened to the journalist, Schramm, who had commissioned the theft, but it wasn't worth investigating. The main thing was that my life had returned to normal. No more criminal investigations, just forensics and the use of DNA techniques in these, described in a book for professionals who had to work with the results of such investigations.

At least, that was my plan.

That night Robert warned me that a criminal could have installed malware on my hard disk. He urged I contacted Tom to have it checked, and have the latest protection software installed. I called Tom for an appointment right away and made an appointment for next week, since Tom was in the middle of exams and was not available earlier than that. I considered the risk small that my computer was hacked, and, not telling Robert about it, continued to use it till Tom dealt with it.

***

I blame an arts exposition for it. It was their advertisement that was posted all over town, with a photo of an abstract painting by one of the exhibiting artists, that forced my thoughts back to the murders. It showed circles in various colours and dimensions, some intercepting, others overlapping. Like cubism, but then round. Circles. Expanding circles. Two expanding circles and then a third, intercepting rather than expanding the others. That vision came back stronger than ever. I couldn't help myself. Although I had promised myself to put it aside, I had no other choice than to continue solving the puzzle.

Once more I called Lea.

"Hi Sue, haven't seen you for a while! Everything all right?" At least she remembered me.

"Yes, there had been other things on my mind so I had to lead a different life for a while." I guessed most of the girls of the club lived in parallel worlds that they kept strictly separate. Again I had to ask Lea a favour.

"As long as you don't ask the impossible again…" she hesitated, but this time it wasn't a difficult thing I needed her assistance for. All I needed to know was if she had ever seen a certain woman in the club?

"I know her real name, but that may not be the name she is using. She is tall, with long red hair, very pretty, gorgeous legs. She is extremely flexible and walks and moves very elegantly, gracefully, as if she dances. You know what I mean?"

"Yeah, sort of… does she have a Bavarian accent?" I had never noticed Janine had an accent, but maybe she could fake one?

"I'm not sure, I mean, she didn't when I knew her in another life, but she may use it in a different environment…" What else could I add to describe her?

"I have done workouts with her in the past, in another gym. She has an excellent condition and I have seen her do the splits without an effort." Would she show that talent in *In Corpore Sano*?

"Yes, that must be Chantal. She said she was from Munich. Tall, long legs, great body, and as you say, very supple, moves like a leopard." It could only be Janine. "She has only been with us a couple of months. Isn't there very often, though," added Lea. She was keen to help a private detective with ongoing investigations, probably enjoying the thrill.

"Great Lea, the thing is, I need to get in touch with her but she has moved, and I have lost her telephone number. Can you do me a favour please? Can you call me when next time you see her at the club?" Of course she would, as long as her name were never mentioned. She had a suspicious nature, a kind of occupational disorder, I guess. I assured her there was nothing to worry about, and I gave her my mobile number again, in case she had lost it.

***

I was frustrated with the new project I had taken on. It was commissioned by a research group who had tested a commercial product that belonged to what is called 'functional foods', a food supplement that was marketed to increase the consumer's health. The commercial producer had paid for the research, which was supposed to show, under controlled, experimental conditions, how effective the product was. Unfortunately, it turned out there was no effect at all, which posed a problem to the Ph.D. student who had analysed the outcomes of the experiments. He wanted to publish his results, as even negative results are worth publishing (though more difficult to get through the review process that is required for scientific publications), but the company would not like his analysis and certainly not his conclusions. His supervisor had asked me for an independent opinion; he had sent me both the draft of the publication and, after my request, the raw data the student had worked with. I had checked the methodology, the data, the statistics and the conclusions. There was nothing wrong with the work, and no other conclusion could be drawn than that the product was ineffective. The supervisor should have made it clear to the company, before agreeing to their financial support, that the outcome of research isn't always what one desires. Better still, he should have insisted on permission to publish the outcome, independent of the results obtained. Now I had to tell him, as politely as possible, that there was no alternative than to confront the company with the conclusions, hoping they wouldn't insist on a publishing ban. I felt sorry for the poor Ph.D. student, who would be dependent on publications to get his degree. I wrote and edited sentences endlessly in an attempt to be both supportive and stern. It wasn't easy and I was tired. I could no longer concentrate.

My thoughts wandered back to the puzzle of the expanding circles.

What had started the whole thing? Actually, it had been Kazinski's denial of Monica's DNA results. And what had been the last event? The presumed but unexplained suicide of his technician and lover. Since then, there had been no further killings. I had not heard of new developments, neither from the press, who no longer showed an interest in the prostitute murders, nor from Braun, who had not contacted me any more. A circle has no beginning and no end. Kazinski was involved in the beginning and in the end of these murders (I still refused to accept Gudrun's death was suicide, but I couldn't be certain hers would be the end). Was Kazinski the clue; was he the key person in this whole thing? Had he started murdering prostitutes and then, like a snake biting its own tail, continued to kill his own lover? His round face with the round spectacles was in the centre of the circles. *Your Eureka moment will come*, Robert had said. It felt I was close to a solution, it was just around the corner, like when a word is at the tip of the tongue. As if only one more connection in my brain needed to be established, two synapses needed to make contact, but I couldn't get there. I turned a corner and another one, never arriving where I was heading for.

I realized I had dozed off when my head nodding over woke me up. I stretched and got up to go to bed. Tomorrow I would finish the letter to my client.

***

Rain lit up in the light of street lamps, a thin, fine rain, more like a mist, that hardly reached the ground. I was waiting outside, wearing a raincoat and trying to stay dry under an umbrella, cursing I hadn't prepared myself well enough. The rain wasn't the problem, but it was so bloody cold! I watched the door of milky glass set in chrome from the other side of the street. Lea had called earlier to say Chantal had arrived. I had cancelled my membership of *In Corpore Sano*, no longer prepared to pay their excessive fee or comply to their rules, so I could not go in. Now I waited outside, hoping Janine wouldn't stay there too long. I was certain she and Chantal were the same person. I resisted the urge to stamp my cold feet. Three times the door had opened already, but it had not been Janine leaving the club. How much longer was I going to wait?

Finally, the door opened again and I saw the familiar, sophisticated moves of Janine as she stepped out.

I crossed the street immediately and started walking in the same direction as she was heading to.

"Hello Janine," I greeted her when I had caught up with her. She looked up, startled, her long chestnut hair waving as she briskly moved her head.

"Sue?" was all she could say once she recognized me.

"Sorry to bump into you like that, but in fact, I was waiting for you." She could see from my wet coat that I had waited quite some time. "Do you mind if I join you for a bit? I need to talk to you." She didn't reply, but as she stepped slightly to the left, to make space for me on the sidewalk, I regarded the gesture as an invitation. I held the umbrella up to cover us both.

I had considered beforehand what I would say once we met. I had practiced this conversation in my thoughts as I anticipated she wouldn't give me a second chance.

"I know you use the name Chantal inside there," I moved my head in the direction behind us. "I was a member of that club myself."

"What? You?" She was utterly surprised, as I was not the typical woman visiting such facilities.

"Well, I wasn't a member very long, and I didn't join them for the reasons others do. I had to get inside the place for an investigation. I recently cancelled my membership, although the investigations aren't finished yet. That's why I want to talk to you. Do you mind? It is rather a long story, I'm afraid." Like Lea and Tini had done before, she asked me if I was working for the police. Her next question was if she was in trouble. We didn't know that much about each other. But having shed more than a few drops of sweat together had created some sort of bond. We weren't complete strangers. I trusted her, to some extent at least, and I tried to assure her that I could be trusted, too. Eventually she agreed and invited me to her place, which was only a few streets away, where we could talk.

# XXVI

Janine took me to her apartment, which was on the third floor of a late nineteenth-century building. With its beautifully decorated entrance, the wooden stairs with carved railings, and the ornamented ceilings, the building clearly reflected the wealth of Germany under Kaiser Wilhelm the second. Inside, her apartment was surprisingly modern, with the exception of the original windows. It was tastefully furnished.

She offered me a drink – I opted for tea to get warm again.

It turned out to be a long visit. After we had made ourselves comfortable, I started to tell her my story. I explained her about my profession, how I got involved in the murder cases of the two girls, Lena and Laila, who had both been members of the club she had joined. How the press victimised Bamberg the politician and Helmuth the Captain-of-Industry, who had also been club members. I briefly described my unofficial collaboration with the police (without mentioning Braun's name). I explained the fake results originally reported by the Forensic Institute, and that the police eventually learned the truth.

My story was not complete, though. I omitted the bit about the nightly break in, as it would only harm the image I was building of myself. She needed to trust me, and since she only partly understood the principles of criminal evidence, it was easy to skip a few details. I also left out the hypothesis of blackmail, as there was no evidence that either press victims had actually been coerced.

The more I told her, the more involved Janine became. She seemed to enjoy herself, and her reserves vanished as my story developed.

I elaborated on the assumption that the hairs that had been recovered from the crime scenes had probably been collected in *In Corpore Sano*, implicating that the killer had access to that facility, too.

"So, as you can see, many leads pointed in the direction of the club, which is why I shortly became a member. I visited it only a few times. I met Lea and Tini, you know them?" Of course she did, the two were always present and inseparable. "I believe they can only be booked together," she commented, forgetting the unspoken code between us that we wouldn't mention the sexual activities related to the place I euphemistically called 'the club'.

"Well, I had asked them for help when at one point I thought I could predict the date of a third murder. But my prediction was wrong, and the girls didn't turn out to be very reliable. They never got back with the information I had asked them to gather."

Janine was not surprised. She didn't have a high opinion of the two, it seemed. I continued my story.

"Instead of a third murder, which I had expected would take place soon, something else happened. A woman appeared to have committed suicide, but I think she was actually murdered. She had been a technician at the Forensic Institute, and she also happened to be the lover of the Director. Her name was Gudrun." I thought it important to mention the names of the dead women. In contrast to Braun, I didn't want to impersonalize them. They had been human beings, women of flesh and blood, grown up in a family and with a past, but no future due to a criminal act.

"So not only do multiple leads point towards the club, there are also multiple clues related to that director, whose name is Gottfried Kazinski. The more I think about it, the more certain I am that he had access to *In Corpore Sano*. But I can no longer go in to check, and since he knows me, I wouldn't want to run into him at the place." She grinned.

"So you want me to check if he is a customer?" She was spot on. Of course I could have asked Steffan if Kazinski's name appeared in the books of the sex club. But he could have registered under a false name, and I was reluctant to contact Braun without being able to offer him something in return. I had accused Kazinski more than once of misdoings, to which Braun had always been sceptical. Right now Janine was a better source of information on club members. I described the looks of Kazinski.

"He could be wearing a hairpiece or something, but his short build and his high-pitched voice will make it easy to recognize him." With that I finished my description.

"I don't think I have seen him around so far, though I haven't spent much time at the club yet," commented Janine. "Do you believe he is the murderer?"

"I don't know. It isn't likely that he killed his lover, is it? And I don't know if he knew the two other victims, that is what I want to find out. I think he had a reason to mess with the data he reported to the police." If Kazinski were identified as a member of *In Corpore Sano*, it would provide a possible connection between him and the murdered prostitutes. But what if Janine would not meet him there? I couldn't ask her to visit the place all opening hours. So a negative was indecisive, but a positive was a hit. Just like in science, sometimes. After a moment of silence, Janine asked:

"Describe me what Gudrun looked like." I had considered it unlikely that she could have been a member of the club, too, but it was a possibility we shouldn't rule out. What if Kazinski had seen her there, discovering a dark side and a secret life of his sweetheart? It could have made him angry, and it could be a reason for murder, to some people. I didn't know if Kazinski was of the jealous type, but finding out your girlfriend and employee works as a prostitute in her spare time isn't a nice discovery. I had only recently experienced how strong feelings of jealousy can influence one's actions.

I recalled Gudrun's looks from the photograph of the lab's team. There wasn't anything remarkable about her, other than her fiery-red dyed hair, done in the out-of-bed style. That wasn't enough for Janine to identify her.

"Maybe there is an obituary on the web about her. That's what people do nowadays," she said, as she rose to switch on her computer that stood at a small desk in a corner of her living room. I spelled out Gudrun's last name and after a few clicks Janine had found a photo of her face.

"Never seen her in my life!" she concluded after a careful look.

"OK, so that is one hypothesis developed and rejected, all in one session. Not bad for a first round!" I commented. We both laughed. I felt I could work with Janine. We parted as friends.

***

Tom was shocked when I told him I had continued to use my computer after it was recovered from a theft.

"Dr. Swanson, you should never have accepted it back! God knows what has been done to it. You are living a dangerous life with this, do you realize?" Now, now, it wouldn't be life-threatening, would it, if some crook had installed the odd worm or virus?

"First of all, your password had been cracked, which suggests there was spyware installed on your computer. It isn't just viruses and Trojan horses, there are all sorts of dangerous programmes out there." He started counting on his fingers: "there is Adware, a type of malware that automatically delivers advertisements that pop up and often lead to Spyware," (his second finger) "software that spies on your computer activity and can collect keystrokes to identify your passwords. That is how someone could have gained access to your hard disk." Suddenly I remembered the strange email that I had received from Thomas Schramm, saying he had checked my website and giving me a dead link to, what I had presumed, would lead to his website in return. How naïve I had been! By clicking on that link I had unknowingly installed spyware on my computer, which had read my keystrokes next time I logged in. I remembered my computer had frozen shortly afterwards. Meanwhile, Tom wasn't finished with his lecture. He continued with a third finger for Bots and Rootkits, software programmes that take over your computer and that unnoticed send out spam or can turn it into a zombie that obeys the illicit scripts continuously. Next, his little finger identified Ransomware, a form of malware that demands a ransom while freezing your system... with every finger his tone became more serious.

"Tom, stop it please, I get it. Yes, I realize I lived dangerously. Can you check if any of these vermin now live in my computer? And if so, can you fix it? I guess you'll find at least one copy of spyware script in there."

"I can try to fix it..." was his uncertain answer. That didn't sound very reassuring. It would require a thorough check, for which I had to separate from my computer once more. Just as I had gotten used to having it back! Oh well, I would manage. Reluctantly I handed over the power supply, feeling abandoned from my baby once more.

"I'll do my best to do it as quickly as possible. I'll give you a call when it is done." With that, I parted from my second brain another time, again feeling guilty and worried.

***

Once more I was admiring the decorated ceiling of her flat. Janine had asked me to come over because there was something to talk about. While she was in the kitchen preparing coffee, I studied her living room in daylight. She had used an interesting combination of colours: one wall was painted light blue and the others were left white. The furniture was a combination of antiques (I particularly liked a delicate Chinese-style carved commode made of a dark type of wood), a modern-style glass dining table with black leather and chrome chairs, and two oversized orange two-seaters, covered with white and light-blue cushions. It made an interesting and tasteful combination. A large painting on the wall opposite the couch I was seated on displayed a sunset, with orange and light blue as the dominating colours. I wondered if it had been that painting (an original, as far as I could tell) that had made her choose these colours for her living room, or whether the painting had been the finishing touch.

Janine came in carrying a tray with an espresso coffee pot and two cups.

"You don't take sugar, do you?" She poured both of us a cup and settled herself, curling up like a cat, on the other couch set at an angle with mine.

"Sue, before I tell you what happened last night, I have to thank you for not criticising what I'm doing for a living. I mean, not everybody agrees with my profession."

I gestured it wasn't worth mentioning. It was no business of mine how she earned her money. As long as there were men who needed their services, there would always be prostitutes. And with her anatomy, she might be able to make a few men a little happier, and earn a good deal of money with hit. It wasn't for me to judge whether this was good or bad. Prostitution was not illegal in Germany, and as long as she had chosen this profession voluntarily, I had no problem with it.

Then she started talking.

Since my launch at her she had visited the club every night of its restricted opening hours, as she didn't want to miss a chance to spot Kazinski. She had even described the looks of him and Gudrun to Lea and Tini, but they couldn't remember seeing a person like her at the place. Then last night something strange happened, which she wanted to tell me.

"It was at the bar, I was talking to a guest, and we were just having a chat, when he mentioned something about lab work. You know how it is, we normally try to get an idea of the profession of a client, so that we can guess their financial status. This guy, he called himself George, was obviously an academic, well-mannered, manicured hands, a good talker. Anyway, I was interested, and I guess he wanted to impress me, because he told me more and more about his work, which had to do with forensics. Just like the stuff you had explained to me. I was glad you had introduced me to the subject, because now I was able to keep up with him without too much of an effort. He seemed to know a lot about it."

I couldn't help asking if she was certain it wasn't Kazinski?

"Oh, definitely! This guy was tall, dark blond with a beard and a low voice. Actually, quite a nice voice he had."

While she continued to report what they had talked about, I was only half listening. I felt a surge of anxiety. I was convinced the killer of Lena and Laila had selected his victims in *In Corpore Sano*. They had both been beautiful women, stylish, not at all the vulgar type of prostitute. Janine was just like them, beautiful, graceful, she would most definitely match his preferred type of prey. Last night she may well have chatted with the killer! And he was knowledgeable about forensics. That fitted as well, the murderer obviously knew how to avoid leaving his own traces at a crime scene, and had deliberately produced false tracks.

Janine had finished her story now, and was waiting for my response. I hadn't quite listened to the last bit she had told me.

"Sorry, what did you say about a brother?"

"Half-brother. I told him Kazinski was my half-brother."

*What??*

"Can you repeat the last bit of your story? I wasn't paying attention to what you said." So when he asked how I knew so much about the subject, I told him I had a half-brother who works in that field. It was just a little lie to keep the conversation doing. But he wanted to know his name, and then I mentioned Kazinski. I think that was a bit stupid, wasn't it? I shouldn't have said that."

"How did he react?"

"There wasn't much of a reaction, really. He said he didn't know that name. But later I started to worry. I though I'd better tell you about it. What do you think?"

There certainly was reason for concern, whether this so-called George knew Kazinski or not.

"Tell me, how did your conversation end?"

"He said he would be in touch. Not sure if he will, but it is possible he'll ask for a rendezvous. Then he left. Nothing unusual happened. But I am still not completely comfortable with it."

I didn't like this at all. I didn't want to scare her in case there was nothing wrong with this man, but what if he was indeed our killer? I couldn't take the risk.

I warned her to be very careful, and to avoid being alone with this person. I made it clear I had suspicions, no certainty, but he could, I repeated, he *could* be the killer.

"Oh my gosh, I'd better stay away from him, then! What should I do? Shouldn't we inform the police?" It was too early for that. We had no evidence of any misdoings. I needed confirmation first. I could imagine how Braun would respond to another of my crazy theories again.

We agreed she would let me know if she saw George again, or if he contacted her. Again I stressed her to be careful. But her profession demanded she frequently had to be alone with men, without the presence of witnesses. I prayed she wouldn't find herself alone in her room with a serial killer.

# XXVII

I wasn't at all comfortable with what Janine had told me. It had been my fault that she had drawn attention to herself from a man who could be dangerous. If I hadn't talked her through some basics of forensics, and if I had not given her the name of Kazinski, she might never have gotten into his gunsight. The more I thought about it, the more certain I was that we had identified our man. Now I felt responsible for the consequences. I would never forgive myself if something happened to Janine. I felt obliged to protect her.

On my way to Tom to collect my computer, I made a mental list of what I needed for this protection. Equipment that would allow Janine to earn her money and still keep her safe, at least, relatively safe. Tom was the only person I knew to ask for assistance. I hated to pull him back into the darker side of society, but I had no idea how else to purchase the things I needed. I had never operated in this branch.

To my relief, my computer was safe and sound, it appeared. Tom had not been able to identify anything of harm, other than a piece of spyware that had sent my keystrokes to the Darknet. That had enabled the wrongdoers to read my password. He had been able to remove the malicious script, but had kept a copy of the IP address to which the spyware had been connected. I was grateful for that; it may help Steffan to build his case against Schramm, who I was certain had been responsible for planting it in my computer. After a thorough check Tom had installed all the latest protection software that was available, updated the latest software versions and had defragmented my hard disk. He explained this was normally not needed with a Mac, but since a number of large files had been stored on my hard disk, it could improve performance. He went on about gigabytes, Flash storage drives and hot file adaptive clustering, until I stopped him, exclaiming I hadn't got a clue what he was talking about. The main thing was my computer was all right. I instructed him to address his invoice to my company, as usual. But I wasn't finished with him.

"Tom, there is something else I need to ask you. It has nothing to do with computers, but I think you can nevertheless help me. Do you mind a moment?"

He listened to my wishes with an expression of disbelief on his face. He probably regarded me as a relatively boring adult, with an uninteresting job, doing unexciting science, a bit of travelling, but nothing he could chill at. He would never have imagined that I could be in need of equipment fit to feature in a James Bond movie.

He interrupted me a few times, asking for details, and then started to take notes.

"The essential thing is: it has to be small. Small enough to fit in a piece of hair accessory. I have brought a couple of examples so you know what I mean." I showed him a collage of photos I had copied from the Internet, with various hairpins, diadems and elaborate hair bands that were big enough to hide electronic equipment in. He inspected the photos with interest.

"And you are sure the thing can connect to a mobile phone?" He nodded: he had written that requirement down already. "Once a connection is established, will I be able to forward it to another number? Without losing the connection myself?"

"That is something I have to organize in the mobile phone itself. It has nothing to do with the sender. But I can do that, that's not difficult at all."

I knew I could rely on him.

"The stuff won't be cheap, though," he commented. I didn't care. The main thing was that Janine would be safe.

"No problem, you just order everything in my name and I'll take care of the payment."

Apparently, that was not how it worked. The Darknet didn't accept credit cards by default.

"In that case, do whatever needs to be done and I'll pay you back in cash." That was more like it.

"But please Tom, don't get yourself into trouble. Your father would never forgive me," I added.

"My father will never find out," he replied with confidence.

***

We were giggling like little girls while I tried out various coiffeurs with Janine's hair. It was not only long but also thick, which required large adornments and multiple strong hairpins to keep it up. That was good, as these pieces provided enough space to hide the equipment Tom had delivered. He had not let me down. Within four days he had called to tell me the 'goods' were ready to collect. We had tested them at his place, checking the batteries and the connection to a mobile phone that he had also delivered. He had explained in excessive detail how it all worked. I said I would rehearse it several times to make sure there would not be any surprises. I could tell he wasn't convinced of my technical skills.

Finally, I managed to get her complete mane stuck up. A last pin to add stability and I was done.

"What d'you think?" I asked, while she inspected her head in the mirror. Like a hairdresser I held a second mirror behind her head, but lacking experience, my angle was wrong and she didn't see anything. She adjusted the back mirror herself and with a smile moved her head left and right.

"It will do, but now the stress test!" she said, and started vigorously shaking her head. The coiffure held.

Then she stood up and went into her bedroom. A few moments later she came back, my careful work ruined. Strands of hair stood out at various angles.

"See, Sue, it has to be stable enough that I can lay down with it. Sorry, we'll need to start over again!" The curse of her profession, I called it.

Eventually, we accomplished tying her hair into a stable construction that withstood every pillow she tried. Now we were ready to test the equipment. She went back into her bedroom and closed the door. I took out the telephone Tom had bought for me, an old-fashioned-looking mobile phone, and waited. When it silently vibrated, I pressed the button showing a green telephone symbol and listened.

"Sue, can you hear me?" Janine's voice was surprisingly clear.

"Loud and clear. What about you?"

"A bit faint, but I can hear you." With that, she re-entered the living room. I disconnected the call, and she stuck a finger somewhere in her hair in an attempt to disconnect the line, too. After a bit of fiddling, she withdrew a large hair clip in which her mobile device was hidden.

"We'll have to adjust the volume of your speaker. You must be able to hear me clearly. Can we move that pin closer to your ear?" I didn't want to increase the volume of her speaker too much. A person in her presence should not be able to hear it, not even if his head was very close to hers.

"Can't you just speak up a little?" That wouldn't do either, as I planned to be in her vicinity, though out of sight. Again, anybody in her presence should not hear me speak. Tom had instructed me how to regulate the volume of her speaker, which was hidden in an elaborately decorated hairpin. The piece was adorned with multiple imitation jewels. The mobile devices that served as a microphone and cell phone was separate from her speaker. Everything communicated by Bluetooth. All equipment was minute, and glued to the back of the hair jewels. I moved the pin bearing the speaker closer to her ear, pointing the speaker more downwards. We tested it again.

"Much better now!" she reported from behind the closed door, clearly audible through my phone. I took pictures of her head from all angles to be sure we could reproduce this construction of hair and clips and pins when it was needed.

There was one more thing to check. Using my own smartphone, I called Tom to tell him we were ready. Janine disappeared in her bedroom again and my second phone vibrated once more. I answered the call again and then pressed a pre-programmed button and listened. I could hear Janine's voice:

"This is me again, can everybody hear me?"

"This is Tom, I can hear you, Roger," I had to smile over his military manner. "Sue here, loud and clear," I responded. Then I talked to Tom through my smartphone, confirming everything worked well. The trial had gone just fine.

***

I hadn't informed Steffan Braun yet. It could have been a false alarm. So far I had no factual evidence that the man Janine had talked to at the bar of the sex club was not just a normal customer. I would not again make a fool of myself in front of the Chief Inspector.

But Janine's message this afternoon changed everything. George had contacted her and had asked for an appointment this Saturday night. She had agreed to meet in the club at around nine. It was Thursday now. I had reassured her nothing would happen to her, as long as we kept to our plan. We had thoroughly prepared ourselves. And I would make sure she would have police protection. It was time I made the call.

Braun was surprised to hear from me, and reluctant to talk to me.

"Steffan, I know I have misled you several times, but this time is different. I have very strong reasons to believe we have identified our killer."

"Who is 'we'?" he interrupted in his matter-of-fact style.

"That is myself and a female member of *In Corpore Sano*. I knew her before she attended that club, and she has described a person who behaved suspiciously, and whom she is going to meet this Saturday night. She needs police protection, as she is just the type this man has killed twice already…" Again I was interrupted.

"Please, not so fast. Do I understand correctly that you are in touch with one of the ladies of that sex club? I thought you had quit your investigations, but even so. We are currently going through the list of members, male and female, and the owners of that club are fully cooperative. They have provided us with all data and all available CCTV records. If I recall correctly, there are currently thirty-five female members, and including those that have cancelled their membership during the past four months, we are dealing with forty-three women. You know their profession. We can't possibly provide police protection for all of them while they…" Now I interrupted him:

"That's not what I am asking, Steffan! I demand protection for one girl in particular. Her name is Janine, but in the club she is known as Chantal. As I said, she is just the same type as the two previous victims were, and she was approached by a man who…"

"And in addition, there are seventy-two male members who are currently being screened. You will have to be patient." He continued his dry statistics as if he had not heard what I had just said. I nearly lost my temper. He wasn't just reluctant, he was bluntly uncooperative!

"Please Steffan, listen to me! You won't find anything suspicious on those tapes. The man behaves just like all other customers. But he knows about forensics, he talked about it to Janine. And then she mentioned the name of Kazinski and now he…"

"How does this woman know Kazinski?"

"She doesn't, she only knew his name." Steffan must have realized I had given her that name. I continued trying to convince him the situation was urgent now.

"It is no coincidence that this man is suddenly interested in her. I believe Kazinski is the clue that connects the murders."

Now Steffan's voice sounded as if he was losing his patience.

"What is it you have against that man? He is innocent. We checked his alibi, he had nothing to do with those murders. I don't understand your sudden panic. The last killing was four months ago, and since then nothing has happened. We are still continuing our investigation, but it no longer has high priority. I can't just reserve my staff to guard a prostitute on one of her dates unless you present me with some very convincing arguments!"

It was hopeless. I played my last card, explicitly asking what I needed.

"I have already given you my arguments. May I politely request the following: can you keep a police car stationary close to the sex club on Saturday night from eight thirty onwards, please? And can you keep your mobile phone with you? You may receive a call from a number I'm going to text you. If that number calls you, just answer it without saying anything. All you need to do is listen. The line will be connected to a microphone that Janine is wearing. You can hear the conversation and judge for yourself whether you consider it necessary to interfere. Can you agree to do that, please?" I was nearly begging now.

He was silent for a moment.

"So you want to bug her? You understand that at some time she may have to part with her clothes?"

Oh yes, we had thought of that. At last it sounded like he was now seriously considering cooperating. Finally he said:

"OK, I can do that. To have a manned car stationed in that area for a couple of hours is not a big deal, I can justify that. But if nothing happens, the action ends at twelve sharp. Is that understood? And you stay clear from the scene!" The last sentence was a command, not a question. I agreed with everything he demanded in return for his help.

"Fine. Do you mind if I call you an hour earlier, that is at seven thirty p.m. on Saturday, just to make sure our arrangement is followed?" He had no objection, though he commented:

"I always keep my promises." I was certain of that, but with Janine's safety at stake, I'd rather double-check.

## XXVIII

"How do you answer 'yes' to a question?"

"Reference to temperature."

"For example?"

"You're so hot. Do you like it hot? You make me hot. I have cold fingers." That last one made me laugh. We were practicing our codes. Our communication would be one-way only. I would be able to hear Janine through the connection to my telephone, but she cold not speak to me directly. She could hear me by means of her hairpin speaker, but if I asked her something she would have to answer in code. For this we had invented various codes with sentences that would not interrupt her activities with the customer.

"And for a negative answer?"

"Anything referring to smell." Before I could ask she added examples: "I like your aftershave. Do you like my perfume? I love the smell of a man. Do you want to smell my…"

"OK, that's fine!" I interrupted. Her vocabulary was limited to the anticipated occasion, with which she was obviously more at ease than I was.

"What is the code for 'I don't know'?"

"I don't know," she replied, and then it was her time to laugh.

"No, I'm joking, I know it: a reference to time. How much time have you got tonight? I wished this could go on forever. If only we could stop the time. How long are you planning to stay? What time is it?"

"What is the code to let me know you're all right?"

"Any reference to my name. I like the way you whisper Chantal. Do you like my name? Will you remember sweet Chantal?" She said all this with a sexy voice and a strong Bavarian accent. It was amazing how she could switch into her role without the slightest effort, while we were comfortably seated in her living room with tea and cookies on the table in front of us.

"Janine, you should have become an actress!" She laughed away the compliment.

"And if things are not all right I will mention the bathroom. Actually I will try to make it to the bathroom so that I can talk freely in there. And if all else fails I'll start screaming."

"No you won't! There will be no reason to scream. It may only cause him to panic. And remember, the police are listening in and they know your codes. So as soon as you mention the bathroom they will storm in. So what will you do if you actually need to use the bathroom?"

"I will just go. I don't need to ask for permission, do I?"

It would do. We had prepared everything as best as we could. I had confirmed the codes with Steffan and had handed him a list with their meanings for reference. Janine would invite George to her apartment, like she usually did with a customer. I would be in the basement, where the laundry room was located. That meant I was in her vicinity while we communicated, but he would never see me. The plan couldn't go wrong.

***

The laundry room smelled of detergent. Every apartment had its own washing machine down here, each connected to an individual water metre. I counted eight, five of them with a dryer on top. One was working and on another one the little LED lamp marked 'END' was on; laundry clung to the sides of the drum. I had inspected all types represented, noticed two identical ones, counted the brands, compared the complexity of laundry equipment collected on each (one machine had no accompanying detergent at all, another bore a basket with eight different bottles and powders). There wasn't much else to do while I waited nevously.

Through the connection to the mobile phone Tom had provided I could hear soft music. Janine was at the bar of the club, waiting for George. We had both vainly tried to hide our nervousness for the other. She was wearing a leopard-print, low-cut (at the top) and high-cut (at the legs) leotard as if to emphasize her feline body, complemented with black stockings and high heels. Over the leotard she wore a short black cape made of silk. The combination was surprisingly stylish. Preparing her outfit, her hair and our equipment in it had taken over an hour. Her coiffure was rigid with gel and hairspray. We had triple-checked all batteries and had connected and disconnected the line multiple times before she left her apartment.

It was a quarter to nine. All we could do was wait. As long as I heard the music I knew she was peacefully (or so it looked) drinking a tonic, which she had ordered without gin. Carlo the barman would be in her vicinity, providing protection in case she needed it.

"Oh, my telephone," she said, and I could tell she was digging it out of her handbag, as the melody of her phone became louder.

"Chantal here," I heard her say, and then, in a sweet voice and using her Bavarian accent:

"Hello George, are you on your way? I'm waiting for you." Silence.

"OK, I'll be outside in ten minutes. No problem. A blue Audi you said? See you soon, bye!" A few moments later I heard a door close and the music stopped.

"Sue, I'm in the, *ehm*, I'm in a room alone right now. He just called me to say he will pick me up with his car outside the club. He said it'll be difficult to park here, and we won't be staying here anyway. So I'll be outside in a minute, OK?"

I couldn't think of anything against this change of plan, so I confirmed this was fine. I had not yet connected her line to the phone of Steffan, but I knew he was on standby and a police car was stationed in the neighbourhood: I had checked with him half an hour earlier.

I heard a door close again, Janine saying goodbye to Carlo and greeting someone, then her footsteps through the corridor towards the exit. Suddenly the loud sound of the wind blowing in her microphone nearly deafened me.

"It is a bit windy, can you turn your head so that the microphone is at the lee side?" The wind stopped and now I could hear traffic noise. "That's better!"

A few minutes later I heard a car horn hoot twice, and she whispered:

"That's him, I can see his car. I'm going in. Wish me luck." Some rustling, a car door closing, and then her voice again:

"Hello George, you look great tonight!" followed by a man's voice:

"And you look fabulous, sweetie," and the soft sound of a car accelerating.

"Wait, I can't buckle - OK I've got it. I'm all right. Are you taking us to Chantal's place tonight? Shall I guide you?" I realized the mention of the name was for me to let me know she was all right.

"I know the address." I could barely hear what he said. We should have put the microphone to the left side of her head, because he was in the driver's seat! It didn't matter; they would be at her place soon. But how did he know...?

"How does he know your address?" I asked my phone.

"How much time will you have for me tonight, then?" she responded. A reference to time. So she didn't know the answer. I couldn't make out the words of his response. It didn't matter. Steffan had guaranteed police assistance till twelve, which was more than three hours from now. If anything was going to happen, I expected it would not take that long to develop.

I noticed I was shivering. *Calm down, Sue, everything will be fine.*

Her voice again:

"We should have turned left here. Are you sure you know the address?" He responded something indiscernible. Then, in a clearer voice:

"Why did you do your hair like that? I prefer to see it loose." He must have turned his head to watch her while he said this.

"It's nice to know your preference. I won't forget." Pause. Then:

"Where are you taking me?"

Her tone had changed, she sounded alarmed. Was she all right? Was he behaving normally? What was he planning, where was he taking her? *Only one question at a time, Sue, a question that allows a clear yes or no answer!*

"Is he behaving normally?"

"It will take a long time to get to my place this way," she said. So she couldn't tell if his behaviour was normal. Again I could hear him clearly:

"Loosen your hair, please. I don't like it that way."

"Do you think he is our killer?" With her experience, she should be able to tell whether a man behaved hornily or had other things in mind. He made comments about her looks, so maybe he was indeed only planning to have sex with her. I needed to know how she judged the situation.

"No worries, sweetie, I will wear it loose next time. There will be a next time, won't there?" A double reference to time. She couldn't tell what his intentions were. My heartbeat was fast now. *Calm down, Sue, she will be all right.*

"Is he taking you to your apartment?"

"I like your aftershave!" was her response. Damn, he was not taking an alternative route, he was not heading for her place at all!

"Is he using a navigator?"

"Do you like my perfume, too?" So he wasn't. I had to act! *Do something!* It was no use staying in the laundry room of her flat if they weren't on their way to her place. I hurried up the stairs and left the building half running.

"Janine, I'm heading for my car. Can you mention the street name where you are driving right now?" Unfortunately my car was parked quite a distance away. I started running faster, the mobile phone pressed to my ear to be able to hear what was happening.

"Why are we on the *Brunnenstraße*? You are not taking me to my apartment, are you? Where are we going?" At least that was something. The street she mentioned was one of the main streets from the south leading into the centre of town. Still running, I panted:

"Are you driving south?"

"It is hot in here. Can you turn down the heating please?" Positive! I finally reached my car. I fumbled with my keys singlehandedly while I tried to concentrate on their location and their possible destination. They had started from the club, so if they were now on the *Brunnenstraße* driving south they could be heading for the motorway. This wasn't going well! I started my engine and dashed off, impatient for my navigator to wake up. Although I was driving in the wrong direction, away from them, I couldn't turn round, as this was a one-way street. I had to inform Steffan: the manned police car that he had stationed close to her sex club was useless now. But George had not actually done anything suspicious yet. He had just changed the location of their date. I heard his voice again:

"Take it off." A loud crack in my microphone. Janine shouting:

"Hey, leave it! I don't want to..." some rustling, then her voice, calmer now, sexy even:

"Why are you so focussed on my hair? Don't you think I have other parts that are more interesting?" and after a short moment: "That's better, I like that."

I heard their car engine going slower and then stop. My navsat was now showing the town map and I had figured out the fastest route to follow them. I couldn't use the route planner as I didn't have a target address, so I used the map function instead, zooming in and out manually to work my way out of the centre of town. Their car drove away again, according to the sound of the engine. Must have been a traffic light.

His voice: “You said you are related to Kazinski?” Why did he bring that up? I clenched the mobile phone between my left ear and shoulder, and, left hand on the steering wheel, pulled my smartphone out of my right pocket to call Steffan; this was now getting more than suspicious. He needed to listen in. The voice from my left shoulder sounded muffled: “It doesn’t matter, sweetie, I don’t want to talk about my family. Where are we going?”

“The thing is, I couldn’t find anything about a half-sister of Kazinski.” I used the shortcut on my smartphone to make the call. Steffan answered immediately. I spoke fast, nearly shouting:

“Things aren’t going well. Janine is in the car with the man and they are driving south, out of town. He has mentioned Kazinski and he just said he knows she isn’t his half-sister. I will connect you to her line now, OK?” He confirmed, and I disconnected quickly. Then I pushed the button on the other mobile phone that would connect him with Janine’s head. At least I was no longer the only person responsible for her direct safety. Janine would have overheard my call, so she knew Steffan was now also connected to her line. I readjusted the mobile phone closer to my ear so that I could hear clearly again.

“So tell me the truth: are you really related to him?” he repeated. Janine kept quiet.

“Are you still driving the *Brunnenstraße*?”

“Why are we talking about this? I want you to be hot.” I checked the map. I had nearly reached that street myself, but they would be ahead of me. I sped up to pass a traffic light; too late, it was red by the time I reached it. Going even faster, I crossed the intercepting road while traffic to my left and right already started to move.

“Who are you? Have you been lying to me?” he asked Janine, and his voice was now openly aggressive.

“You know who I am. I need to pee. Can we stop somewhere please?” She didn’t mention Chantal, the name he knew her by. She clearly stated her message to me and Steffan that things were not going right. What could we do?

Another crack in her microphone. Her voice screaming: “No don’t, you’re hurting me. Don’t...” A loud crack, and then nothing. Silence. The sound of the car engine was gone.

“Janine I can’t hear you. Can you hear me?” No reply. I repeated my question again and again. Nothing. Damn! Either the line had gone completely dead, or the microphone that recorded the signal for my phone was no longer working. Maybe he had pulled at her hairband, in an attempt to loosen her coiffure. I didn't know if she could still hear me, but without her being able to communicate to me I had no clue where they were going.

I abruptly stopped my car at the roadside. *Think quickly now, Sue!*

# XXIX

*'If anything goes wrong, call me.'* That was what Tom had said. I knew he was on standby. At this moment I hoped he could do more for Janine than Steffan could. I called him immediately on my smartphone and he answered without delay with a short 'yes?' only.

"Tom, it has gone wrong. The man has taken her in his car and they are driving towards the south of town. My connection is lost. I don't know if she can still hear me, or whether her line to the police still exists. What to do?"

"If you can't hear anything, the police won't either because the signal is transmitted through your mobile. Give me a second." I heard him typing on a keyboard.

"I'm sending you a link to your smartphone. Open this and it will show GoogleMaps, with the cursor showing. I'll hang up now." I switched to my email and opened the new message from sender 'Tom.computer.service'. I clicked on the link. While the screen was popping up, the mobile phone on the passenger's seat rang. It was Tom.

"Does it work?" On my smartphone a blue dot in the middle of a map was visible. It stood still on *Brunnenstraße*.

"Yes, I can see the dot on the map. What am I looking at?"

"I had a GPS built in in the hairband. It sends its location regardless of the telephone connection. I just linked its signal to your smartphone. So as long as the hairband is in the same car as the woman, you can trace her. You hadn't asked for this but I considered it worth the extra money." It certainly was! I could kiss him for his inventiveness.

"The dot is starting to move again. I'm going after them. Will keep you posted!" and with that I disconnected him and raced off again, keeping an eye on the blue dot on my smartphone in case they changed direction. I passed another red traffic light and was now doing over one hundred kilometres per hour, while I was still driving within town. If I were caught it would cost me a few points at Flensburg, the national register for traffic violations. I risked losing my driving license for three months. I didn't care.

The smartphone in my hand rang; it had to be Steffan, who wanted to know what was happening, but I couldn't answer him. I needed the map to know where George was aiming for. The ringing stopped.

I grabbed the other mobile phone in an attempt to call Steffan from that line, but I was unable to dial while driving at this speed in an urban area and at the same time keeping the smartphone in my hand. I threw the mobile back on the passenger seat with too much force: the stupid thing slid off into the space between the seat and the passenger's door. Damn, it was now out of reach as long as I was driving, and I needed my smartphone to follow the blue dot, which was now crawling towards the motorway access. There was no way I could inform Steffan what was happening. I compared the map of my navsat that showed my own position with the Googlemap that identified George's car. I was making progress. They weren't so far ahead of me anymore.

I put my foot down on the accelerator, my left fist clenching the steering wheel, my other hand holding the smartphone while stabilizing the wheel. A sign above the road indicated the motorway was five kilometres away. The dot on the phone was approaching the access lane. Even faster I accelerated. Fortunately there wasn't a lot of traffic on the road right now. Ahead of me I could see the signposts that counted the metres towards the access: three white stripes for three hundred metres. Two white stripes for two hundred. I would have to slow down in order to turn right.

But wait, the blue dot had stayed on the road, it wasn't entering the motorway! Ahead of me I saw the rear lights of a car. I checked the two screens again: although the maps were different representations, and my navsat had zoomed out automatically in response to my high speed, it appeared the symbol of my own car and the blue dot were in the same position. I needed to slow down now and threw the phone away in order to steer properly with two hands. I had used my brakes with too much force: my foot felt the pulses of the anti-lock braking system controlling my traction.

I was now close enough to the car in front of me to see it contained a passenger. Closer still and I saw the four intercepting circles of the Audi logo. I activated my blinker and started to move to the left. I would be able to overtake them before the next traffic light.

I was still behind the car when its left blinker lighted up. The car was starting to move into my lane, apparently preparing to take a left turn at the next junction. I had to react quickly. I put my foot down on the gas as hard as I could. The sound of screeching tyres. My car jumped forwards.

I hit the left rear of the Audi with a bang, trying desperately to keep control of my vehicle. I noticed I started spinning and while I hit the brakes a fist hit me in the face. The sound of metal crunching. By the time the airbag had deflated and I had recovered sufficiently from its blow my car had stopped at an angle to the road; my left hind end had hit the guardrail. To the right of me a dark blue car stood motionless, hissing, ridiculously close to where I was. My right front had entered its hind flank, boring itself inside.

Dizzy and in shock, I managed to open my door. My trembling right hand felt burned and blood trickled from my face. The passenger door of the other car opened and slowly a woman with untidy long red hair appeared.

"Janine, you all right?" I shouted. The person on the driver seat didn't move. His head hung on his breast. While Janine leaned on the car to support her legs, I moved towards the driver's door to check. It was severely mangled and wouldn't open. The driver was still motionless, his trimmed beard touching his breast. Blood dripped from his face onto his white shirt. A bald patch was visible on the back of his head.

"Janine, keep an eye on him, please. I'm going to call the police."

A lorry had stopped behind us and a man climbed out in a hurry, to see how he could help.

"Please help the woman," I shouted. "Don't touch the driver!" I couldn't be sure if he had not broken his neck. While I moved back to my car, which looked like a wreck, more cars stopped behind us. Our collision had blocked the left lane completely and part of the right lane as well.

"Can someone secure the place please? Put a warning sign up!" I shouted, then I tried to get a hold of my smartphone that was lying on the floor of my car somewhere. Several people pulled out their phones to dial 110. Instead, I dialled the shortcut to Steffan's mobile.

"There has been an accident. I'm OK and so is Janine, but the man is unconscious." I gave him our location. At a distance I could already hear the siren of a police car.

Finally, I collapsed in the arms of Janine, both of us in tears.

***

We were seated in Steffan's office. My wounds had been treated by the paramedics and weren't too serious. Surprisingly, Janine had not been hurt at all. George had been taken to hospital by an ambulance, still unconscious, but it had been confirmed his neck wasn't broken. The police officer who had taken control over the accident site had been utterly surprised when Steffan had arrived, in his private car with a temporary blue light fitted to its rooftop. He had identified himself and said he would take over the interviews, as the accident was now considered a crime scene related to multiple murder cases. Members of his team had closed the road completely and had taken photographs from every angle. Eventually, after consultation with the medics, Steffan had driven us to his office. A junior uniformed officer had joined us.

I hadn't yet called Robert to tell him my car was wrecked. It was past two o'clock in the morning now and I didn't want to wake him up. I granted him the sleep of the ignorant; by the time he heard about my adventure he would be in enough stress.

Janine had begun to tell her story. A tape recorder on the table in front of us ensured her words were properly documented.

"After he pulled at my hair I heard Sue say she couldn't hear me. I answered her but she repeated she couldn't hear me. I realized he had disconnected the microphone somehow."

"Do you think he realized you were bugged?" I dared to ask, although I wasn't the person supposed to ask questions. Steffan didn't seem to mind.

"Not sure, he kept going on about my hair. Maybe he really didn't like it being tied up? Anyway, when I realized I was disconnected I started to panic. He had asked about my relationship with Kazinski. He knew I wasn't his half-sister." Braun nodded. We had still been able to hear that part of the conversation. What happened then?" he asked. Apparently, George had stopped the car on the side of the road and, after pulling at Janine's hair, he became aggressive.

"He grabbed my wrists and pushed them down hard, on my lap, so I could barely move. He said I needed to tell the truth. So I said I had only mentioned the thing about Kazinski being my half-brother because I wanted to impress him. I was really scared! He let go of my wrists and said I wasn't important to him anymore. That I was a nobody. I was only of interest to him if Kazinski had been family of mine, that's what he said. Then he started the engine again and continued driving. I don't know where he wanted to take me." She looked terrible. I wished I could put an arm around her and comfort her but the interview wasn't over yet.

"Do you mind if I take over?" I asked Steffan. He nodded. Then I told him what I had discovered after the accident. I had had enough time to connect the dots. I could have known it all this time, if only I had made a bit more effort. I finally had had my *Eureka* moment.

"The man's name is Günther Müller. *Doktor* Günther Müller. He used to work at the Forensic Institute. I recognized him after the accident. He was a member at *In Corpore Sano*, where he used the name George. I had seen him at that place once, a couple of weeks ago. I believe he murdered two female members of that club and had placed false evidence at the crime scenes in an attempt to defame Kazinski. He had hoped to become director of the Institute but Kazinski got the job. Müller not only lost his position, he was never able to find another, so his career was shattered. I guess that's why he held a grudge against his competitor." My feeling was that initially he only wanted to kill once. Placing three different hairs would obviously pose a problem to Kazinski, who would have to report this unlikely result to the police. Müller had made certain one of those hairs was from Bamberg, who also visited *In Corpore Sano*. However, the official press release never once mentioned the existence of conflicting forensic evidence. Müller probably wrote the anonymous letter to Dornfeld, disclosing the link to Bamberg the politician, in an attempt to put pressure on the case, but Dornfeld took his time publishing that information.

So when the letter didn't have enough effect, Müller decided to kill again, making certain this time Kazinski would be in trouble, with two hairs from different individuals again, recovered from a similar crime scene. That also backfired, as the police remained of the opinion (at least, according to their press releases) there was no connection between the two murders. A letter to the second journalist, Schramm, revealed the connection to Helmuth, and indeed the circles started expanding. But contrary to Müller's plan, the person of Kazinski never got into the picture.

So Müller decided to hurt his enemy directly. He must have found out about the love affair with Gudrun, and strangled her with the rope that he then hanged her with, leaving her as if it had been suicide. Maybe he had stalked her, and had waited for a suitable occasion. It certainly helped that Kazinski had visited her shortly before her death: it nearly put the police on the wrong lead. That was how Gudrun's circle intercepted the expanding circles of Lena and Laila: Kazinski had been at the interception. If only I had paid more attention!

I explained my theory as best as I could. I was absolutely certain it was the truth, although I couldn't prove it. Janine watched me with eyes wide open and an expression of horror on her pretty face. Maybe only now did she realize in how much danger she had been. Steffan remained calm, as he always did.

"When Janine mentioned to Müller that Kazinski was her half-brother, he realized he could hurt his target once more, and he arranged a meeting with her. But in the car he found out it had been a lie. That's why he said he had lost interest in her." Steffan remained silent for a moment. He finally commented:

"An interesting hypothesis, Dr. Swanson, but unfortunately it is impossible to prove any of this."

"Wait a moment!" cried Janine. "I haven't told you everything yet. George, or Müller, or whatever his name is, said he would not make his hands dirty on a nobody like me. '*you're not worth killing for again*' is what he said. Literally, that's what he said!" Her voice trembled as she repeated those terrible words. Steffan was not impressed.

"Frau Schwarz, it will be your word against his. There were no witnesses to this conversation. This will never hold in court. I can't arrest the man based on this testimony." He sounded highly disappointed. Looking around the table to check everybody had said what they wanted to say, he officially closed the interrogation for now and switched off the tape recorder.

This couldn't be! We had solved the case, we knew Müller had murdered three women, surely we couldn't just let him go like that?

# XXX

It was just then that a thought struck my mind. All I needed was one phone call to find out if there really was no evidence. I asked for five minutes in private, and went outside.

It took less than five minutes. They hadn't even left the room by the time I got back. I asked Steffan to switch the tape recorder back on.

"I have just spoken to an expert about the wiretap equipment that has been used tonight." I would try to keep Tom out of this if I could; so far I had not mentioned his name at all. "I now have confirmation that all communication of tonight is stored on a microchip. Provided the microphone wasn't damaged, the last bit of the conversation that took place in the car before I... before the unfortunate accident, will have been recorded." I had woken Tom up with my call – after the accident I had informed him all was well, and he had gone to bed. But now he had told me the equipment he had supplied had been expensive for a reason: it had come with every function you could possibly need for illegal activities, including automated recording. Tom considered it likely that the connection to my phone had been damaged, rather than the microphone itself. With a bit of luck, Müller had said one sentence that could put him in jail, and that sentence had been recorded.

***

It turned out we had been lucky that night.

Müller was eventually charged for multiple murders, all three of which he confessed to. He was arrested while he was still in hospital, recovering from a severe concussion. The only charge he got away with was attempted murder, as it couldn't be proven that Janine had been in real danger. The craziest part of his story was his explanation of the hairs: by leaving these on the scenes he had wanted to ridicule Kazinski's baldhead. How sick can a person be?

My car was totalled, which I regretted as I had been very fond of it. The police provided assistance in my correspondence with my insurance company, until they reluctantly accepted the accident had not been my fault, despite the fact that I had hit a car from behind. I didn't get a lot of money back, though, as my poor car had served me quite a few years already, and wasn't worth much anymore. Oh well, there are less important reasons to buy a new car!

Janine and I stayed friends, although I warned her that I was not very good at keeping friendships. She said she would be as persistent as a mosquito. I could live with that.

My biggest surprise was the reaction of Kazinski. He had been so shocked about the whole thing that he took sick leave, and eventually quit his job. Somehow I felt sorry for him: he had been the centre of the crimes without even knowing it.

And my book? I finished it, the publisher was happy and I was proud of the result, but it didn't sell as many copies as I had hoped for. I hadn't expected otherwise: the science behind forensic investigations is far more boring than the crimes they try to solve.

Made in the USA
Charleston, SC
09 January 2016